M.C. Beaton worked as a Fleet Street journalist. She is the author of the Agatha Raisin novels, the Hamish Macbeth series and the Edwardian Murder Mystery series – all published by Constable & Robinson. She divides her time between Paris and the Cotswolds.

Praise for M.C. Beaton's Edwardian Murder Mystery series:

'If you missed the first novel in the series, get it right away. *Snobbery with Violence* introduced the Edwardian heroine Lady Rose Summer. Her second appearance [*Hasty Death*] is, if anything, even wittier and more amusing than the debut.'

The Globe & Mail

'Fans of the author's Agatha Raisin and Hamish Macbeth series should welcome this tale of aristocrats, house parties, servants, and murder.'

Publishers Weekly

'A light-hearted romantic romp through Edwardian snobbery, with hints of the cataclysmic changes in store for high society.'

Kirkus Review

'An amusing brew of mystery and romance that will keep fans turning the pages.'

Publishers Weekly

'Fans of the author's Hamish Macbeth and Agatha Raisin mysteries ... will welcome this new series of historical whodunits.'

Booklist

'Combines history, romance and intrigue, resulting in a delightful romantic mystery.'

ID0818358

HASTY
DEATH

M.C. Beaton

ROBINSON

Constable & Robinson Ltd
3 The Lanchesters
162 Fulham Palace Road
London W6 9ER
www.constablerobinson.com

Published in the US by St Martin's Press, 2004

This paperback edition published in the UK by Robinson,
an imprint of Constable & Robinson Ltd, 2010

A copy of the British Library Cataloguing in Publication data is
available from the British Library

ISBN: 978-184901-290-4

Typeset by TW Typesetting, Plymouth, Devon

Printed and bound by CPI Group (UK) Ltd, Croydon, CR0 4YY

5 7 9 10 8 6 4

To George and Isabel Agrest of Paris,
with affection

Shorthand he wrote, his flower in prime did fade,
And hasty death shorthand of him hath made.
– Epitaph of William Laurence,
died 1661, Westminster Abbey

CHAPTER ONE

Don't, when offered a dish at a friend's table,
look at it critically, turn it about with the spoon
and fork, and then refuse it.

Etiquette for Women,
by one of the aristocracy

Winter is very democratic. In London, its grip extended from the slums of the East End to the elegant squares of Belgravia. Tempers were made as brittle as ice by the all-encompassing cold, even in the home of the Earl and Countess of Hadshire. Their London home in Eaton Square had run out of coal and wood. The butler blamed the housekeeper and the housekeeper blamed the first footman, and as the row about who was responsible raged downstairs, upstairs, a battle royal was going on over a different matter.

Lady Rose Summer, daughter of the earl and countess, was once more demanding to be free to work as a typist. Not only that, she wanted to move to some business women's hostel in Bloomsbury with her maid, Daisy.

The previous year, the earl had thwarted a visit from King Edward VII by employing a certain Harry Cathcart who had blown up a station and a bridge to convince the king that if he visited the Hadshire country estate, the Bolsheviks would assassinate him. Now Rose was threatening to make this public if her parents did not agree to her wishes.

Wrapped in innumerable shawls and a fur tippet where dead little animals stared accusingly at Rose, her mother, the countess, Lady Polly, once more tried to let her daughter see sense. 'For one of us to sink to the level of trade would be a social disaster. No one will want to marry you.'

'I don't think I want to get married,' said Rose.

'Then you should have told us that last year, before we wasted a fortune on your season,' roared the earl.

Rose had the grace to blush.

Lady Polly tried a softer approach. 'We are going to Nice. You'll like it there. Sunshine, palm trees, very romantic.'

'I want to work.'

'It's the fault of that ex-chorus-girl maid of yours,' raged the earl.

Daisy Levine, Rose's maid, was indeed an ex-chorus girl. She had come to the Hadshires to masquerade as a servant with typhoid, an initial plot by Harry Cathcart to deter the royal visit. Rose had taken her under her wing, taught her to read and write, then to type, and then made her a lady's maid.

'It is my idea, Pa,' said Rose. 'We've argued and argued about this. My mind is made up.'

She walked from the room and closed the double doors behind her very quietly – much more effective than if she had slammed them.

'What are we to do?' mourned the earl, huddling farther into his bearskin coat, looking like a small, round wounded animal.

They sat in gloomy silence. The doors to the drawing-room opened and two footmen entered, one carrying coal and kindling and the other a basket of logs.

'At last,' said the earl. 'What took you so long?'

'There was such a shortage of fuel in the city, my lord,' said the first footman, 'that we sent two fourgons out to the country to Stacey Court.' Stacey Court was the earl's country home.

'Well, get the fire started,' grumbled the earl.

As the resultant blaze began to thaw the room, the earl felt that even his brain was beginning to thaw out. 'I know,' he said. 'We'll ask that Cathcart fellow. What's he doing now?'

'Lady Glensheil tells me he has opened a detective agency. Very American. Like Pinkertons.'

'I'll try anything,' said the earl. 'We could have left for Nice a week ago if it hadn't been for Rose.' He rang the bell and told the butler, Brum, to find the direction of Captain Harry Cathcart's detective agency and ask him to call.

Harry Cathcart brightened when a footman brought him the earl's request. It was not that time had been lying heavily on his hands. On the contrary, his days were taken up, just as before, with hushing up society's scandals and finding lost dogs. But he had hoped for more dramatic assignments, and somehow, working in the past for the earl had certainly led to murder and mayhem.

He picked up his hat and coat and went through to the outer office where his sheep-faced secretary, Miss Jubbles, was labouring over accounts.

'I'm going out for a bit, Miss Jubbles,' he said. 'Anything I can get you?'

'Oh, no, Captain.' Miss Jubbles gazed adoringly at the handsome captain with his thick dark hair, rangy figure and black eyes. Harry shrugged himself into his fur-lined coat and crammed a wide-brimmed hat on his head. Out in Buckingham Palace Road, where he had his office, the cold was intense. In a neighbouring building the pipes had burst, and icicles glittered against the sooty brick. Other buildings had lagged the outside pipes with old sheets and he felt he was walking past ghostly sentinels with their whitish arms stretched up to the frost-covered roofs. He walked carefully because the street-sweepers had been unable to clear the pavements of the frozen-hard mud and it was slippery underfoot.

As he made his way to Eaton Square, he felt a frisson of excitement. He would see the infuriating Lady Rose again. He remembered her as he had last seen her with her intense blue eyes and thick brown hair, her figure unfashionably slim in this new Edwardian era, where men liked their women plump.

At the earl's house, the butler took his hat, coat and stick and informed him that Lord and Lady Hadshire would see him in the drawing-room. Harry mounted the stairs behind the butler thinking the earl must really have some major problem or he would have received him in his study.

'Come in, come in,' cried the earl. 'Sit by the fire. Sherry? Yes? Fetch the decanter, Brum. You been shooting, Cathcart?' He surveyed Harry's tweed coat, knickerbockers, thick socks and brogues.

'No, I do realize I am unfashionably dressed but my attire is suitable for the cold and I gather you want to see me on business.'

'Yes, wait until we get the sherry and I get rid of the servants.'

'Where is Lady Rose?'

'In her room,' said the earl gloomily, 'and let's hope she stays there.'

Daisy turned away from the window as Rose entered her private sitting-room. 'I just saw Captain Cathcart a few minutes ago coming into the house.'

'What on earth is he doing here? Oh, no! Pa's probably asking his help. But what can Cathcart do?'

'Get a tame doctor to say you're mad,' said Daisy. 'Then you'll be put in a lunatic asylum and I'll be sacked.'

'They wouldn't do that,' said Rose with a nervous laugh.

'It would solve their problem. If you then said anything about that plot to stop the king visiting, no one would pay you any attention.'

'If they do that, I will run away.'

'We could do that anyway, my lady.'

'No, they would put advertisements in all the newspapers and I would be hunted down. Oh, what on earth are they talking about?'

'It's all very simple,' said Harry when the earl had finished.

'How?' The earl goggled. 'I'm not having her put in an insane asylum. I know that's the thing, but she'd never get married and I want grandchildren. A boy. Who's going to inherit, hey?'

'I am sure Lady Rose would be competent to run your estates.'

'A woman? Never!'

'Very well. What I suggest is this. I have a friend, Mr Peter Drevey, a merchant banker. I can persuade him to employ both Lady Rose and Daisy as typists. You will have to pay him a fee to cover wages for both, and for his discretion.'

'If the fellow's a gentleman, he won't want to be paid.'

'If he is paid, then I can get him to sign a confidentiality document. I am sorry, my lord, but I have outstanding accounts because I was naïve enough to take the word of a few gentlemen. Then both ladies may move to a business women's hostel. I suggest you do not pay Lady Rose an allowance and her clothes must be limited to those of a woman in her adopted station. By the time you return from Nice – two months, you said – you will find her more than eager to come home. I will keep a discreet eye on both of them for you. You will forgive me for asking for my usual fee in advance, I am sure.'

'A thousand pounds? Oh, very well. But I want you to put the matter to Rose yourself. I've had enough of her tantrums.'

'Very well.'

Rose was summoned to the drawing-room. She stood in the doorway and surveyed the captain. Lady Polly thought for one moment that the very air seemed to crackle between them, but put it down to the cold working on her imagination.

'The captain has something to say to you,' said the earl. 'He has my blessing.'

A faint blush suffused Rose's beautiful face. So Harry had asked for her hand in marriage! Well, she wouldn't accept, but still . . .

Her parents left the room. 'Pray be seated,' said Harry.

Rose sank down gracefully into an armchair by the fire. He sat down opposite and a little frown creased her brow. Shouldn't he be getting down on one knee?

'I have come up with a solution to your problem,' began Harry.

'I do not wish to marry,' said Rose, but she gave him a little smile and her long eyelashes fluttered.

'Of course you don't,' said Harry cheerfully. 'You want to be a working woman and I am here to help you.'

Rose's face hardened with disappointment. 'What is your plan?' she asked.

Harry outlined his idea but without saying that the merchant banker would be paid to employ her, merely saying he knew of two typing vacancies at the bank.

'And my parents agreed to this?' asked Rose faintly.

'Yes, they are anxious to leave for Nice.'

'I suppose I must thank you,' said Rose, feeling depressed. It was one thing to dream, another to face going out in the cold winter to work.

'Very well. If you come across any difficulties, please let me know. My card.'

Rose felt an odd impulse to burst into tears as she took his card.

'Remember, you must be sure not to betray your real rank. You must wear ordinary clothes and be known simply as Miss Summer. And modify your accent. I am sure Daisy will tell you how. I suggest you buy cheap clothes. I am sure that even your oldest ones will betray your rank. No furs.'

'And if I refuse?'

'Then you will be a good daughter and go with your parents to Nice, and then, I suppose, to India, which is the destination these days of all failed débutantes. Your parents do not seem too anxious to pay for another season.'

'You are blunt, too blunt.'

'I call a spade a spade.'

'Indeed! Are you usually so cliché-ridden?'

'Good day to you, Lady Rose.'

'Infuriating woman!' said Harry to his manservant, Becket, when he returned to his Chelsea home that evening.

'Do you think Lady Rose will actually go ahead with

it, sir?' asked Becket, placing a decanter of sherry and a glass on the table next to Harry.

'Oh, I'm sure she will. Stubborn as a mule!'

Daisy chewed her thumbnail and glanced nervously at her mistress. If the weather hadn't been so cold! Also, she had become used to lavish meals and pretty clothes. And to think that she had almost persuaded Rose to go to Nice after she had learned that Captain Cathcart intended to holiday there. But the captain had cancelled his plans for a vacation, becoming embroiled in setting up his new business. Daisy thought the captain would make Rose a very suitable husband, and she herself was fond of the captain's servant, Becket. Her face lit up as an idea struck her.

'I saw the captain's advertisement in *The Tatler* the other day. He's just started that detective agency. Maybe he needs a secretary. Be more exciting than working in a bank.'

'What a good idea!' exclaimed Rose. 'And I could help him to detect like I did last year. We will go out tomorrow to say we are looking for working clothes and we will go there instead.'

On the following day, Miss Jubbles looked up from her typewriter at the beautiful creature facing her flanked by her maid. 'May I help you?' she asked.

'I am Lady Rose Summer. I wish to speak to Captain Cathcart.'

'I am afraid Captain Cathcart is not here. What is it about, my lady? I can take notes.'

'That will not be necessary. I am here to offer my services as a secretary.'

Miss Jubbles looked at her in horror. Then her sheeplike face hardened and the two hairs sticking out of a large mole on her chin bristled.

'But he does not need a secretary. I am his secretary.'

'But the captain and I are friends,' said Rose.

Miss Jubbles rose to her feet. This spoilt beauty was trying to take her job away from her.

'I work here,' she said, 'because I need to work for money, not on a whim. You should be ashamed of yourself, trying to take the bread out of my mouth. Get out before I throw you out!'

Daisy moved forward, her eyes blazing. 'You and who else?'

Rose strove for some dignity. She put a restraining hand on Daisy's arm. 'I made a mistake,' she said. 'Come, Daisy.'

Half an hour later, Harry came back. 'Fog's coming down, Miss Jubbles. Anyone call?'

Miss Jubbles gave him an adoring smile. 'No one at all, sir.'

'Right.' Harry went into his office.

Miss Jubbles looked possessively around her little empire: her meticulous files, her kettle with the bone-china cups arranged beside it, the tall grimy windows, the battered leather sofa and the presence of the adored boss behind the frosted-glass inner door. All hers. And no one was going to take it away from her.

* * *

Rose would not admit to Daisy or even to herself that she was frightened. Pride would not let her back down. After the disastrous visit to Harry's office, of which she was now thoroughly ashamed, they went to Bourne & Hollingsworth in Lower Oxford Street and Rose began to choose suitable ready-to-wear clothes for both of them. Rose had never worn ready-to-wear clothes in all her young life. Ladies did not.

Daisy advised her that they should limit their wardrobes to two tweed costumes for winter and two serviceable lightweight dresses for summer. 'Well, we don't need to buy new underwear,' said Rose. 'We can wear what we've got. No one's going to see that!'

'Unless whoever runs the business women's hostel decides to snoop in our rooms,' pointed out Daisy.

'We'll take one of the old steamer trunks, one with a good lock on it,' said Rose, 'and use that for underwear. Surely I can take one fur coat?'

Daisy shook her head. 'Tweed with a bit of fur at the neck is all we can get. Two pairs of boots and two pairs of shoes. Two felt hats and two straw.'

At last all their purchases were wrapped and ready. 'Send them to . . .' Rose was beginning when Daisy screamed. 'What is it?' demanded Rose.

'I've lost my bracelet. I think it's over there.'

Rose made a noise of impatience and followed her across the shop. 'You can't have them sent to Eaton Square,' hissed Daisy.

'Oh, yes I can,' said Rose and marched back. 'Send my maid's clothes to this address,' she said, producing her card.

'You are too cautious,' she admonished Daisy when one of the earl's carriages was bearing them home.

'You can't be too careful, my lady,' said Daisy.

'And you had better begin by practising *not* to call me my lady.'

'I think I'd better find that business women's hostel for us myself,' said Daisy.

'Why? I think I should decide on our accommodation.'

'You're still too grand. You can't go arriving anywhere in a carriage with the earl's crest on the panels and dressed in furs. Let me do it.'

'Very well,' said Rose after a show of reluctance to hide the fact that she was relieved. A weak little Rose Summer, deep inside her, was beginning to wish she had never wanted to be a working woman.

Miss Harringey, proprietor of the Bryant's Court Hostel for Businesswomen, ushered Daisy into what she described as her 'sanctum', an overcrowded parlour on the ground floor, stuffed with furniture and framed photos, and where a small yellow canary in a cage looked out dismally through the barred windows at the London fog which was beginning to veil the streets.

Daisy was wearing one of the tweed suits purchased that day under a tweed coat with a beaver-fur trim. She was aware of Miss Harringey's small black eyes studying her and wished she had bought second-hand clothes instead. Daisy's own clothes back at Eaton square *were* mostly second-hand, but they were clothes that her mistress had usually worn only once and had taken a dislike to. She was sharply aware that what to Rose had been cheap clothes might look rather new and expensive to Miss Harringey.

Miss Harringey was a very solid woman, so corseted that she appeared to be wearing armour under her jet-covered woollen gown. Her face was large and heavy and her eyes disproportionately small. Her hair, an improbable shade of auburn, was worn in an Alexandria fringe.

'I would like to make it plain, Miss . . . er . . .'

'Levine.'

'Miss Levine. We only take ladies of impeccable reputation here.'

The clothes, thought Daisy – she thinks I might be a kept woman, as if a kept woman would want to live here!

'I can assure you,' said Daisy primly, 'that me and my friend, Miss Summer, lead very hard-working lives. No gentlemen callers, I can assure you.'

'And where do you work?'

'At Drevey's Merchant Bank in the City. We're office workers.'

'I expect payment in advance.'

'How much in advance?'

Miss Harringey said, 'Three months.'

'All right,' said Daisy.

'I have one double room available at the top of the house.'

'Can't we have separate rooms?'

'None are available.'

'I'd better see this room.'

'Follow me.'

And so Daisy followed Miss Harringey up a narrow flight of stairs to the top of the house. There was a mixture of odours: gas, disinfectant, dry rot, baked potatoes, baked beans, and sour milk. And the all-pervasive smell of cabbage. 'No cooking in the rooms,' said Miss Harringey as she reached the top of the stairs. Daisy sniffed the air and wondered how many of the tenants obeyed that law.

'This is it.' Miss Harringey threw open the door.

In the middle of the room stood an iron bedstead covered in thin, worn blankets. There was a rickety dressing-table by the window with a chipped marble top which held a china ewer and basin decorated in fat roses and a mirror. The 'wardrobe' was simply a recess with a curtain over it. A table and two chairs stood by the grimy window. There was a small gas fire.

'The bathroom is two floors down at the end of the passage,' said Miss Harringey. 'You will need two pennies for the meter, and the bathroom is not to be used after ten at night.'

Daisy walked into the room. She crouched down before the mirror and adjusted her hat. Her rather protruding green eyes in her small face stared back at her.

Rose will hate this, she thought. Good, it might bring her to her senses.

'I'll take it.'

'In that case, we shall descend to my sanctum and I will give you a receipt.'

* * *

14

'Oh, good work,' said Rose when Daisy returned with the news of the room.

'It means we'll need to sleep together,' warned Daisy.

'Oh, things will be fine.' Rose had overcome her fears and was now looking forward to the new adventure. 'I have received a letter from Mr Drevey. We are both to start work next Monday. Eight in the morning until five-thirty in the evening. We are each to receive fifteen shillings a week.'

'Won't go far,' cautioned Daisy. 'Not after what you've been used to.'

'You have paid three months' rent in advance, have you not? So we will have thirty shillings a week between us. We have our clothes. We can eat cheap food.'

'That Miss Harringey said there was to be no cooking in the rooms, but from the smell of the place, I don't think anybody pays any attention to that.'

'The smell?'

'Well, it does smell a bit. But that's life on the lower side. I mean, it isn't as if we have to stick at it, now does it?'

'We must stick at it. I'll wager that horrible Captain Cathcart is laying bets at the moment that we won't be able to last the pace.'

'He wouldn't do that. I don't know why you are so agin him.'

'Against,' corrected Rose. 'He did not even have the courtesy to acknowledge our visit.'

'Stands to reason. That old frump of a secretary

doesn't want to lose her job. She probably never even told him.'

'Oh ... well, no matter. We'll probably be very happy in our new life at Drevey's bank.'

Rose had expected her parents to be worried, but they seemed quite cheerful as she and Daisy packed up what they would need that weekend. She did not know that the earl had already called on Harry and had given him the address of Rose's hostel or that Peter Drevey had promised to give Harry weekly reports of their daughter's well-being. They were also cheered by the captain's belief that Rose would not last very long in her new life. But mindful of the fact that they did not want Rose returning to Eaton Square in their absence, to be minded only by a maid whom both the earl and countess distrusted, they refused to give her a set of keys to the town house.

Mildly hurt, Rose said loftily that she would not need them.

The weekend finally arrived. Lord and Lady Hadshire seemed indecently cheerful as they supervised arrangements for their journey to Nice. Rose was feeling even more uneasy about her new venture. She had rather hoped that her parents might shed a few tears and beg her not to go ahead with the scheme so that she could capitulate gracefully.

But at last her luggage, along with Daisy's, was placed on the outside steps – two suitcases and one large steamer trunk – while a footman fetched a hack.

If this were a novel, thought Rose sadly, as the hack jerked forward, my parents would be waving a tearful farewell from the steps. The farewell had taken place half an hour earlier in the drawing-room and had taken the form of a stern lecture.

At last the hack turned down a narrow back street in Bloomsbury, Bryant's Court.

'Is this it?' asked Rose nervously.

'This is it,' said Daisy. 'I hope they gave you money to pay for this hack.'

'I still have some of my pin-money left,' said Rose.

The cabbie thanked her so effusively and said, 'Good day, my lady,' that Rose was alarmed.

'He recognized me!'

'Nah!' said Daisy. 'You tipped too much.'

The delighted cabbie had carried their luggage to the front door. Daisy rang the bell. The door opened and Miss Harringey stared at Rose.

'Don't expect me to help you up the stairs with that luggage,' she said. 'Come into my sanctum and I'll give you your keys.'

Rose stood nervously while Daisy collected two sets of keys, one each to the front door, one each to the room.

'Miss Levine knows the way,' said Miss Harringey.

Rose was too depressed to say anything. Inside her head, a voice was crying, 'What have I done? Oh, what have I done?'

They decided to carry the suitcases up first and then return for the trunk. Their suitcases were light because they contained nothing but their 'working clothes', but the trunk was heavy because it was not only packed with underwear but piles of books which Rose considered essential and Daisy thought were a waste of time and energy.

Daisy unlocked the door to their room. 'There you are,' she said cheerfully. 'New home.'

Rose bit her lip. She would not cry. But the sight of the room depressed her so much that she felt a lump rising in her throat.

She forced herself to say, 'I suppose it will do. Let's get the trunk.'

Miss Harringey, hands folded on her rigid bosom, watched curiously as they struggled back up the stairs, carrying the trunk between them. Rose turned on the first landing and saw her watching and gave her a haughty, glacial stare. Miss Harringey sniffed and retreated to her parlour.

When they laid the trunk in a corner, Rose straightened up and looked around again.

'There are no curtains,' she said.

'That's 'cos we're at the top of the house,' said Daisy. 'Nobody can look in.'

'I want curtains,' said Rose. 'Good, lined curtains.'

'You do that, and then the old bat will become suspicious if she starts snooping around. Look, we'll buy some cheap ones.'

'And a vase for flowers. I need fresh flowers.'

'My lady . . . I mean Rose . . . you'll need to get used to the new life.'

'A cheap vase and cheap flowers,' said Rose stubbornly.

'There aren't any cheap flowers in winter.'

'We'll get a vase anyway and prepare for spring. But curtains, right now. Run down and get us a hack.'

'People like us don't take carriages,' said Rose patiently. 'We'll walk up to Lower Oxford Street, and then, if you're tired, we'll take the omnibus, and not first class either.'

Rose sat down on the bed. 'Perhaps we shouldn't rush into things. Light that fire, Daisy. This room is abominably cold.'

'I need a penny for the meter.'

Rose opened her handbag and took out her purse. 'Here's a penny. I suppose we'll need to save a stock of pennies for the fire and the bath. Oh, we can't even have a cup of tea.'

'Yes, we can!' said Daisy triumphantly. 'You packed books, I packed essentials.' She put a penny in the meter and lit the gas. She unlocked the trunk and pulled out a small kettle, a teapot, a packet of tea and a paper twist of sugar. 'No milk, but we can have it without. I've brought a pot and frying pan as well.'

Rose began to laugh. 'Anything else?'

'Six sausages and two rashers of bacon and a loaf of bread.'

'But how on earth can you cook?'

'See!' Daisy pulled out a gas ring from the side of the fire. 'I'll put the kettle on.'

Rose began to feel almost cheerful. Daisy lit the gaslight and made a pot of tea. She wondered if Rose realized that a hostel which boasted gaslight *and* a bathroom was above the common order.

19

'I am such a fool,' said Rose. 'When I saw this shabby room, I almost wanted to run back to Eaton Square and hammer on the door and say I had made a dreadful mistake. We will go out and find somewhere to eat and then we will spend the evening in practising our Pitman shorthand. I wish to surprise Papa by making myself indispensable to the bank. I wonder what the other women will be like?'

CHAPTER TWO

O, how full of briers is this working-day world!

William Shakespeare

The alarm clock rang shrilly at six on Monday morning. Rose felt she had not slept at all. Daisy snored, Daisy cuddled up to her during the night, making Rose feel suffocated.

'Wake up!' said Rose. 'Time to get ready.'

Shivering, she lit the gas fire and the gaslight in its bracket by the door. 'I'll use the bathroom first.'

They had both had baths the night before, fearing they would not get a chance in the morning, but Rose wanted hot water to wash her face. She reflected as she lit the geyser over the bath, which exploded into life with a roar, that two pennies in the meter just to wash one's face was already beginning to feel like wanton extravagance. The bathroom was a dismal place. The bath itself was a deep coffin of a thing, but fortunately it was now clean, she and Daisy having had to scrub it out the night before. She washed her face and then

21

filled the jug from the bedroom with hot water and climbed back up the stairs.

'Brought you some hot water,' said Rose.

'What for?' asked Daisy. 'We washed last night. Help me with my stays.'

Rose tied Daisy's stay ribbons and then hurriedly began to dress. 'The bank's in Lombard Street, Daisy. How do we get there?'

'We walk.'

'But it's so far!' wailed Rose.

'I'll find out about omnibuses, or maybe we can get an underground train.'

'I know,' said Rose. 'We'll take a hack and get him to stop just short of the bank. Just this once.'

'Oh, all right,' said Daisy. 'But we have to try to live within our means.'

There were two types of typists in the City – the working girls who were struggling to better themselves, and the middle-class ladies who worked for pin-money.

The senior 'girl' was Mrs Danby, a thin, acidulous woman in her forties. She was middle-class and ruled her small staff of four typists with a rod of iron. Mrs Danby was not looking forward to the arrival of two newcomers, even though it was increasing her empire.

Mr Drevey had told her they were to be put in a separate room and made to type out the entries from the old ledgers. Mrs Danby pointed out that the ledgers were filled with meticulous copperplate handwriting and therefore did not need to be typed and the usually courteous Mr Drevey had snapped at her to do as she was told.

The doorman informed her of the newcomers' arrival and she swept out in the hall to meet them; the only thing modifying her temper was the rustle of her new and expensive taffeta underskirt.

The two newcomers stood before her, irreproachably dressed. 'I am in charge of you,' she said, a surprisingly loud voice emanating from her thin figure and thin trap of a mouth.

'Pleased to meet you,' said Daisy, holding out a gloved hand. 'I am Miss Daisy Levine.'

Mrs Danby ignored the hand. Common-genteel, she thought. Her eyes turned on Rose, who was standing patiently.

'And you are Miss Summer?'

'Yes,' said Rose calmly, fixing Mrs Danby with a blue stare.

'Come with me.' Mrs Danby rustled off in front of them. She threw open a mahogany door revealing a small room furnished with a table, two chairs, a desk, and two typewriters and a pile of ledgers and box files. There was a small gas fire with a broken piece of asbestos which purred and hissed like some infuriated household cat. On the mantelpiece was a black marble clock with a yellow face. By the long window stood a hat stand.

'You are to type the entries in these ledgers,' instructed Mrs Danby, 'and when you have completed each page, you will put it in one of these box files. You, Miss Summer, will start with the 1901 ledger and Miss

23

Levine with the 1900 ledger. Take off your coats and hats and begin immediately.'

Rose and Daisy took off their coats, hats and gloves, and sat at their typewriters, facing each other.

'We need typing paper, if you please,' said Rose.

Rose had intended to modify her accent but she had taken a dislike to Mrs Danby and so her tones were the glacial, staccato ones of her class.

Mrs Danby opened the door and shouted, 'Miss Judd!'

A small girl with a head of black curls appeared. 'Typing paper for these two new workers,' ordered Mrs Danby.

She turned away. Miss Judd winked at Rose and Daisy and shot off to return in a few minutes with a large packet of typing paper.

'I will now watch you to assess your skill,' said Mrs Danby.

Rose and Daisy, like two machines, each put a sheet of paper in their typewriter, found the right ledgers and began to type with great speed and ease.

'I will leave you now,' said Mrs Danby majestically.

'One moment, Mrs Danby,' said Rose. 'At what time are we allowed to take our luncheon?'

Mrs Danby longed to tell them that they were to work right through the day but feared that the haughty Miss Summer might report her to Mr Drevey.

'Luncheon is at one o' clock until two-thirty,' she said.

'Blimey,' said Daisy when Mrs Danby had left. 'It's better than I thought. They do themselves well here. A whole hour and a half for lunch!'

'This is *make* work,' said Rose. 'There is no need for these ledgers to be typed.'

'May as well get on with it,' sighed Daisy. 'If we're awfully good, they might give us some real work.'

They worked hard and their shoulders were sore by lunchtime.

'I need to use the you-know-what,' said Daisy.

'There will be one at King William Street underground station. I read about it in the newspaper.' said Rose. 'I do not want to see more of Mrs Danby than I need to.'

As both were still wearing the undergarments that ladies wore, they spent a considerable time in the toilets.

For the fashionable lady of the day wore an incredible amount of undergarments. To begin with, there was a garment known as combinations: a kind of vest and pants in one piece, made of fine wool, or a mixture of wool and silk, its legs reaching to the knee. It had a back panel which unbuttoned below the waist. Over this went the corset, usually made of pink coutil, boned and shaped to provide the fashionable hour-glass figure. Then came the camisole, a kind of underblouse that buttoned down the front, was gathered at the waist and trimmed with lace round the neck and the diminutive puffed sleeves.

The knickers had lace frills at the knee and they were made from very fine material such as lawn, nainsook or nun's veiling. Silk stockings were clipped to the corset. Then the large round petticoat was placed in a circle on the floor and stepped into.

The only advantage of all these layers of clothes, thought Daisy, when she and Rose emerged once more into the freezing air, was that they kept you warm. Rose had been pleasingly impressed by her first visit to a public toilet and thought it well worth the charge of one penny. It was spotlessly clean and all shining white tiles and polished brass and the female attendant had been courteous.

Daisy stopped at a tobacco kiosk and asked the girl for a packet of cigarettes and directions to somewhere cheap to eat. She told them there was a Lyons a little way along Cheapside.

'You're never going to smoke!' exclaimed Rose.

'I feel like it,' said Daisy stubbornly.

In Lyons teashop, Rose exclaimed over the cheapness of the items on the menu. 'Just look, Daisy, meals are only threepence or fourpence. We could eat out every day! What will you have? There's poached egg on macaroni, Welsh rarebit, or sardines on toast.

'I'll have poached eggs on macaroni,' said Daisy. Rose ordered Welsh rarebit.

'That's better,' sighed Daisy when they were finished. 'We didn't have time for breakfast.'

'It wasn't much to eat,' said Rose, looking around the restaurant and thinking that at home she would have had a choice of eight courses at least. 'It's not as if it's expensive. I never saw this one – braised loin of mutton with carrots. Only sixpence, too.' So they had the mutton with bread and butter, two slices at a penny each. And when they had finished that, they rounded off their meal with coffee, twopence a cup, and apple dumpling, four pennies each. When they finished and Daisy was complaining that she would need to loosen her stays when they got back to the office, they left the cosiness of the teashop with its white-and-gold frontage feeling sleepy with all they had eaten.

As they headed back to the office, the day was so dark that the street lamps were being lit, a man with a long brass pole moving from lamp to lamp and leaving a chain of lights behind him.

The air was not only cold but smelt of innumerable coal fires.

Mrs Danby was there promptly at two-thirty to make sure they were at their desks and then retreated.

After an hour, the door opened and a young man came in. He had a thick head of hair, liberally oiled with bear grease, a long nose and large mouth, and wore the City uniform of black coat and striped trousers.

He affected surprise when he saw them and said, 'Wrong room. But I'd better introduce myself. I am Gerald King.'

'I'm Daisy Levine and my friend is Miss Rose Summer.'

Gerald perched on the edge of the desk, his eyes on Rose.

'You're new, aren't you?'

'Very new,' said Daisy. 'First day.'

'You enjoying it?'

'Not much.'

'Doesn't your friend have a voice, Miss Levine?'

'I do,' said Rose, 'when I am not being kept off my work.'

Gerald retreated. But during the afternoon, several bank clerks found an excuse to drop in.

'You shouldn't freeze them all off,' complained Daisy. 'One of them might buy us dinner.'

'You are not in the music hall now,' said Rose severely.

'No, I ain't,' replied Daisy gloomily.

On Thursday, Mr Drevey went down to the country 'on business', which meant he was escaping to attend a house party.

On that same Thursday, one of the directors, Mr Beveridge, sent for Mrs Danby, and told her that his secretary was ill and he needed someone to take dictation.

'I will bring someone to you directly,' said Mrs Danby.

She decided to select Rose. Rose was too hoity-toity. She would have to confess she could not take dictation and that would bring her down a peg.

But Rose merely asked for a notebook, and that having been supplied followed Mrs Danby up the broad staircase to Mr Beveridge's office on the second floor.

Mr Beveridge was a fat jolly man. Rose was initially unnerved because she was sure she had met him before but he did not seem to recognize her.

Two people were disappointed at the end of the day. Daisy because men popping into the room took one look, saw Rose wasn't there and retreated. And Mrs

Danby because Mr Beveridge had given her a glowing report of Rose's prowess and of her excellent Pitman shorthand.

By Friday evening, Daisy thought she would die of boredom. The evening and weekend lay ahead. It was all right for Rose. She would probably sit reading.

Daisy's days as a chorus girl at Butler's Theatre began to take on a rosy glow. She missed the jokes and the raucous company. And men had found her attractive when there was no Rose to compete with.

In the evening, they cooked sausages over the little gas ring by the fire. Then Rose settled down to read.

'Pity we've got to work tomorrow morning,' complained Daisy.

'Only until twelve-thirty, then we're free,' said Rose, looking up. 'We can go to the British Museum.'

Daisy thought rapidly. 'I might go and see my family if you don't mind being left on your own.'

'Don't promise them all your money. We get paid tomorrow.'

'Naw. Just say hullo.'

Next day, Rose was exhilarated to receive her first pay packet. But she made a mental note to ask for more money if she was going to continue to be employed as a secretary.

She said goodbye to Daisy outside the bank. 'I'll be back this evening,' promised Daisy.

Rose had discovered an omnibus which would take her to Holborn and from there it was an easy walk to her diggings. Conscious of the need for thrift, she paid for a third-class ticket. She did wish people did not smell so bad. Not that the upper classes were so terribly keen on baths, but they did bathe occasionally. Rose took out a small lace handkerchief scented with Parma Violet and held it to her nose.

Daisy felt she was breathing the air of freedom when she stood outside Butler's Theatre in Whitechapel. She was back home among familiar sights and sounds. She had no intention of visiting her family. Although she sent them money when she could, she could not forget her last visit the year before, when her drunken father had tried to assault her.

Daisy was studying the posters when a male voice said. 'Think of going in, miss? It's a good show.'

Daisy swung round. 'Why, it's Billy Gardon!' she exclaimed.

Billy goggled at the sedate little figure in front of him. 'Daisy, is that you?'

'It's me all right.'

When Billy, a comedian, had last seen Daisy, she had brassy blonde hair and thick make-up, not to mention garish clothes.

'What happened to you?'

Daisy grinned. 'It's a long story.'

'Tell you what,' said Billy. 'I got this little flat at the top of the theatre. I'm not on till this evening. Let's you and me go up there and have a glass of hot gin.'

Daisy hesitated only a moment. Telling herself that she'd never had any trouble from Billy before, she let him lead her round the side, through the stage door and up through the inner recesses of the theatre.

She could hear someone on stage singing 'When Father Papered the Parlour' and the audience joining in the chorus.

Slapping it here, slapping it there, paste and paper everywhere,
Mother was stuck to the ceiling, the kids were stuck to the floor.
I've never seen such a bloomin' family so stuck up before!

'Here we are,' said Billy, panting a little as he came to a halt before a door at the top. He swung it open and ushered Daisy in.

She found herself in a frowsty little room. There was a bed against one wall with the blankets spilling over onto the floor. A table against the window was covered with the remains of breakfast. It was flanked by two kitchen chairs and a dead aspidistra in a brass bowl on the window-ledge. The walls were covered in music-hall posters.

Billy cleared the table by lifting up the four corners of the cloth, bundling everything up and putting it in a corner. There was a coal fire spilling ash onto the grate. 'Soon get a fire going.' Billy raked out the ashes, giving Daisy a view of his large plaid-covered backside. Billy was a thickset middle-aged man with a large walrus moustache. His hair was dyed black and his face was red from too much drinking.

When the fire was lit, he thrust a kettle full of water on it, and then opened a cupboard and brought out a bottle of gin and two glasses.

'We'll have some hot water for the gin in a trice,' said Billy. 'Now, let me look at you. What you been and gone and done to yourself?'

He was a good listener. Daisy would not confess to herself that she still found Rose's company rather intimidating. The class lines were strictly drawn. To want to move out of your station was flying in the face of Providence. Everyone knew that God put you in your appointed station.

So it was a relief to be back with what she naïvely thought of as 'her own kind'. Mellowed by hot gin – several glasses of it – she told Billy everything, only forgetting to say that Rose's parents had gone abroad.

'So this earl's daughter's living in this hostel! Where did you say it was?'

'It's at Number Twenty-two Bryant Court in Bloomsbury. Fact is, I'm amazed she can stand it after all she's been used to.'

'Here, have another gin.'

'Shouldn't really. Still, it's a cold day.'

'Run out o' gin. Be back in a mo'.'

Billy raced down the stairs and round to the pub with the empty bottle, which he got filled with gin. Then he went into the chemist's next door to it and bought a bottle of laudanum. His brain was racing. Here was his passport to freedom. No more shows, day in and day out. He was getting on in life.

That evening, Rose was feeling tired. She was also hungry, but there was no sign of Daisy and she wondered whether she should start eating without her.

At nine o' clock, there was a knock on her door. Rose opened it. Miss Harringey stood there. 'There is a person downstairs to see you.'

Rose arched her eyebrows. 'I do not see persons, Miss Harringey. What does he want?'

'I do not approve of gentlemen callers. Would you be so good as to descend and send him on his way.'

Rose followed her down the stairs. 'He is in my sanctum,' said Miss Harringey, throwing open the door.

Rose stared at Billy, from his dyed greased hair down over his plaid suit with the brown velvet lapels to his brown boots, and then her eyes travelled back up again to his face.

'Yes?'

'I am Mr Billy Gardon. You may have heard of me.'

'No. State your business.'

'It's a delicate matter,' said Billy, looking at Miss Harringey. 'It's about Daisy.'

'Step outside with me,' said Rose. 'Thank you, Miss Harringey.'

She led Billy out into a small hall and closed the door behind her on Miss Harringey's curious face.

Miss Harringey opened the door a crack. She heard Billy saying, 'Miss Levine's been taken ill. She's at the theatre. I got a flat there, up top. She's asking for you.'

'I will get my coat and come with you directly,' said Rose.

Captain Harry Cathcart was enjoying his breakfast on Sunday morning when his manservant, Becket, announced, 'Mr Matthew Jarvis to see you on urgent business.'

'Mr Jarvis?'

'The Earl of Hadshire's secretary.'

Harry felt a sudden stab of unease. 'Show him in.'

Matthew strode into the room, his normally pleasant face white with strain. 'I came to you directly. I normally don't work on Sundays, particularly with his lordship being away . . .'

'Sit down, Mr Jarvis. Coffee?'

'No, thank you. I decided to work this morning because I planned to visit my mother in the country tomorrow. I was going through Saturday's post and found this. It had been delivered by hand.

Harry took the cheap envelope and extracted a piece of lined paper. He read: 'If you want to see your daughter again, bring five thousand guineas to Jack Straw's Castle in Hampstead on Monday at two in the afternoon. Don't tell no one or she's dead.'

'Jack Straw's Castle – that's that pub on Hampstead Heath, isn't it?' asked Harry.

'Yes. Oh, what are we to do?' wailed Matthew. 'If the police are informed, it will all come out that Lady Rose was working for a living and she will be socially damned for the rest of her life!'

'Leave it with me,' said Harry. 'Becket, get my hat and coat and come with me.'

'So,' said Harry, when he and Becket were confronting Miss Harringey half an hour later, 'you will understand that as Miss Rose's brother, I am anxious to find her. I have but recently returned from Australia.'

'Some vulgar man called on her. Miss Summer took him into the hall and closed the door on me. As I am a lady, I do not listen at doors.'

'It must be very hard for you, taking care of these young ladies who lodge here,' said Harry.

'I do my best, sir.'

Harry slowly pulled out a rouleau of guineas and extracted five. He then let the gold coins slide slowly from hand to hand. 'I am prepared to pay for information. Perhaps one of the other ladies . . .?'

Staring at the gold, Miss Harringey said, 'I did manage to hear a few words.'

'Which were?'

'I wasn't really listening, but they had left my door open a crack. He said he was Billy Gardon. He said Daisy had been taken ill at the theatre. He said he had a flat at the top of the theatre.'

What a lot of information for someone who wasn't really listening, thought Harry cynically. He placed the five guineas on the edge of a lace-covered bamboo table. It must be Butler's Music Hall. Daisy used to work there.

Rose and Daisy were lying side by side on the narrow bed, bound and gagged. Tears of weakness spilled down Rose's cheeks. Her thoughts had only been for Daisy when she had entered the room ahead of Billy and had seen the still figure of Daisy lying on the bed. As she bent over her, Billy had charged and knocked her flat on the bed over Daisy's body and, pinning her down with his great bulk, had tied her wrists. Then he had gagged her and tied her ankles as well and shoved her on the bed after he had bound and gagged the drugged lady's maid as well.

Daisy kept twisting round to look at her with pleading eyes, but Rose was so furious with her she would not even acknowledge her presence.

Poor Daisy was feeling frantic. Billy didn't know the earl and countess were abroad. What would happen when he didn't get a reply? She had forgotten about the earl's secretary. Rose would fire her after this. She would need to return to the old life – the former life with all its poverty and dirt and squalor that she had so conveniently forgotten. If only they could get out of this, if only Rose would forgive her, then she would get back to that bank and type till her fingers fell off with sheer gratitude.

Far below from the street came the sounds of hawkers and the rumbling of carts over the cobbles, the clip-clop of horses' hooves, and an occasional burst of drunken laughter.

If only I could save us, thought Daisy, then maybe Rose would forgive me. Billy had kept away from them as much as possible. He had not stayed in the frowsty little room during Saturday night. He had visited them on Sunday morning and had lit one candle because the morning was dark and foggy. Thoughtful of the bastard, sneered a voice in Daisy's head.

Then, as she looked at the candle, she had an idea. She rolled over Rose's body and fell on the floor. She rolled across the floor until she was at the wall and, manoeuvring herself until her back was against the wall, she began to push herself upright. Then she jumped across the room to where the candle stood burning on a rickety table. Jumping round until her back was facing it, she stretched her bound wrists over the flame. The pain was excruciating but Daisy held her wrist steady until the rope began to singe and then burn. At last she was able to free her wrists. She tore off her gag and bent and untied her ankles.

She rushed to the bed and ungagged and untied Rose. 'Don't say a word till I use the chamber-pot,' said Daisy, pulling that receptacle out from under the bed. She squatted down while Rose crawled stiffly out of bed. 'I bin holdin' it in all night,' said Daisy, reverting to her former Cockney accent under the strain of it all.

'How do we get out of here?' asked Rose coldly.

Daisy tried the door.

'It's locked,' she wailed.

'He's coming back,' said Rose, hearing footsteps on the stairs.

Daisy seized a frying-pan from a shelf and stood by the door. 'I'll whack the bleeder wiff this the minute he comes in.'

There was a banging on the door and a familiar voice shouted, 'Open up or I'll break the door down.'

'Captain Cathcart!' shouted Rose. 'Break the door down. He may be back any minute.'

The door heaved and shuddered as Harry threw his weight on it and it finally crashed open.

Rose flung herself into his arms and then almost

immediately withdrew, her face flaming. 'How did you know where we were?' she asked.

'Becket will explain. Becket, take the ladies to my home and telephone Mr Jarvis to bring round a change of clothes for Lady Rose and for Miss Levine. I will wait for this Billy Gardon.'

'I can't see our coats or hats,' said Rose, looking around. 'Probably sold them,' said Daisy.

Becket hustled them down the stairs to where two urchins were guarding the captain's car. He tucked them in with fur rugs and then got into the driving seat.

There was a long silence and then Daisy said in a little voice, 'I'm sorry.'

'What came over you, you stupid girl?' said Rose in glacial tones.

Daisy could only hang her head. Her wrists were so painful, she wanted to scream.

'I will set you up somewhere,' continued Rose, 'and then never want to see you again. Do I make myself clear?'

'Yes, my lady,' said Daisy. She wanted to cry, but she had cried so much during the night that she felt there were no tears left.

At Harry's home in Water Street in Chelsea, Becket made tea for them. Daisy whispered to him, 'Can I sit in the kitchen? And have you anything for my wrists?' She held them out.

'Come with me,' said Becket. He led her downstairs to the kitchen and searched in a first-aid box until he found some burn ointment, gently applied it and bandaged her wrists.

'How did this happen?' he asked. 'Did that monster . . . ?'

'Naw,' said Daisy wearily. She told him about burning the rope from her wrists.

'Lady Rose should be kissing your feet, not firing you,' exclaimed Becket.

'I can't blame her. She's had a bad shock. That's why I'd better stay down here where I belong.'

Billy Gardon nipped up the stairs to his theatre flat, dreaming of riches to come.

He stopped short when he saw the door hanging on its hinges. He rushed into the room.

A man stepped out from behind the broken door, swung him round and smashed a fist into his face.

Billy fell on the floor and, nursing his jaw, stared up into the blazing eyes of his attacker. He saw a tall well-dressed man with a handsome face. The glaring eyes were black and hooded. Billy thought he looked like the devil himself.

'On your feet!' roared Harry. 'You blackmailing little worm!'

Billy crawled onto his knees and then stood shakily on his feet, nursing his jaw.

'It was only a bit o' a joke, guv,' he whimpered.

Harry pulled a chair up and sat down. He looked broodingly at Billy. If he turned him over to the police, he felt sure it would leak out to the newspapers. It would come out that Rose had been working as a typist and consorting with an ex-chorus girl from one of London's lowest music halls and her social future would be ruined. And surely a few more weeks at the bank and living in that dreadful hostel would bring her to her senses.

He came to a decision. 'Pack up,' he ordered. 'My man will call on you tomorrow with a steamship ticket to Australia – steerage. If he does not find you – let's say at ten tomorrow morning – I will go to the police. At the least you will get a life sentence of hard labour for this. You will keep your mouth shut. You will not tell anyone. I have spies all over London,' lied Harry. 'How do you think I found you so easily?'

'I'll go, guv, honest. Just give me a chance.'

'Very well. But if any word of this gets out, I shall find you and kill you, and then, I think, report you to the police, who will bury you in quicklime. I do not see why the state should pay for your incarceration.'

When Harry returned home, Becket informed him that Lady Rose was taking a bath and putting on clean clothes. Miss Levine was in the kitchen – 'But I think a doctor should be called to look at her wrists.'

'Why?'

Becket told him how Daisy had engineered the escape.

'Call a doctor. What is Daisy doing in the kitchen?'

'Lady Rose says she wants nothing more to do with her.'

'Let's see about that.'

CHAPTER THREE

*As to making a companion of a servant or
inviting her to the drawing room to have tea with
one, as I have heard is sometimes done, such a
thing is simply ruinous to the mistress's authority
in her own household and highly derogatory to
her personal dignity.*

Mrs C. E. Humphry,
Etiquette for every day (1902)

Harry waited patiently until Rose reappeared, bathed and dressed. 'Thank you for all you have done,' said Rose. 'Have the police arrested that dreadful man?'

'I am making arrangements to ship him off to Australia and I have frightened him into silence. Otherwise society would be delighted to hear of your latest escapade.'

'Being kidnapped and tied up can hardly be described as an escapade.'

'Granted. But the daughter of an earl working in an office would most certainly be regarded as an escapade.'

'You are right,' conceded Rose. 'But what was the point of bringing us here?'

'You need to present a respectable appearance before you return to that hostel. You will tell Miss Harringey that you were both the victims of a practical joke. I told her I was your brother, therefore it will seem perfectly in order for me to escort you back. Now to the problem of Daisy. I gather from Becket that you do not wish to have anything to do with her.'

Rose raised her eyebrows. 'Of course not. How can you even ask such a question? She put my life at risk. I could have choked on that gag.'

'Nonetheless, you might still be choking on that gag if she had not severely burnt her wrists in helping you to escape. Becket has sent for the doctor. You did thank her, I hope?'

'I did not know her wrists were burnt,' said Rose. 'I will see that she is amply compensated when my parents return.'

'Money solves everything, heh? And how will you explain the reason why Daisy must be paid?'

'They will be so glad that I am rid of her, they will pay anything.'

'You are at fault, you know.'

'How, sir?'

'You chose to step outside your class and befriend an ex-chorus girl from the East End. It amused you to do so. You educated her and introduced her to a better way of life and now you want to throw her back again like some toy that had failed to work.'

'That is not the way it was. We were friends.'

'A friendship easily broken.'

Rose's lip trembled. 'I have suffered an ordeal, I am abominably hungry, and yet all you can do is rail at me over a servant.'

'Aha! So Daisy is nothing more than a servant. I suggest we have her up here and ask her to explain what drew her back to her old haunts.'

Harry rang the bell. 'Becket, fetch Miss Daisy. Is the doctor coming?'

'He will be here shortly.'

A few moments later, Daisy was led into the parlour. 'None of us has eaten, Becket,' said Harry. 'A late luncheon, I think, after the doctor has left. Pray take a seat, Miss Levine.'

Daisy sat down on the edge of a chair and Rose turned her head away.

'I am interested to know what took you back to your old neighbourhood,' said Harry gently. 'First, some brandy for Miss Levine, Becket. She is looking extremely pale.'

He waited until Daisy took several sips of brandy.

'Now,' he prompted her.

Daisy gave a dry sob, like a weary child. Rose turned her head and looked at her, at the white face and the bound wrists.

'My lady and I were working in a room together, sir, typing out stuff from ledgers. We decided they were just making work for us. Then one of the bosses needed a temporary secretary and Ro – I mean my lady, got the job. So I was on me . . . my . . . own. Men kept dropping in for a bit, but when they saw it was only me they left.

'I began to feel that Daisy Levine was really nothing. I began to remember the old days in the theatre, where I was considered attractive. I thought I'd just go back to my own kind, as I thought of them. That's where I met Billy. I'd known him before, and when he asked me up to that flat for a drink, it seemed all right to go.

'Like a fool, I told him the whole story. I was lonely, you see. You can't break the barriers of class, sir. It's flying in the face of nature.'

Harry turned to Rose. 'You inadvertently broke the barriers of class, Lady Rose. You joined the suffragettes and then abandoned them. You cannot go around changing the rules and expect things to be easy. So do you want to get rid of Miss Levine and return to your comfortable and privileged life?'

Rose thought of her pride in her job and how she had dragged Daisy along with her into this new life. She remembered Daisy's gallantry, her spirit, and realized for the first time that she would not have been able to go through with the business of getting a job without Daisy.

'I'm sorry, Daisy,' she said. 'Thank you for helping me to escape. We will go on as before . . . as friends.'

'Thank you, my lady.'

'Rose, please.'

'The doctor is here,' said Becket.

'Take him through to the back parlour. When he is finished, we will have lunch.'

'Very good, sir. Miss Levine?'

* * *

44

The doctor declared the burns to be bad but not serious. Daisy's wrists were once more treated and bandaged. She was made to swallow two aspirin and told to rest.

After the doctor had gone, Becket produced a meal he had ordered from a restaurant in the King's Road.

During the lunch, Rose suddenly said, 'I am glad now we decided to work at the bank. Please apologize to your secretary for trying to take her job away from her.'

Harry raised his eyebrows. 'I beg your pardon?'

'I had this mad idea that it might be fun to work for you and I went round to offer my services.'

'Miss Jubbles said nothing of this to me,' said Harry. 'I wonder why.'

'Well, she wouldn't, would she?' remarked Daisy. A touch of colour had returned to her cheeks.

'Why not?'

'She doesn't want to lose her job.'

'Miss Jubbles should have known her job is secure.' Harry's black eyes studied Rose's face. 'I am interested to know why you wanted to work for me. I was under the impression that you neither liked nor approved of me.'

'Daisy and I were of help to you over that murder at Telby Castle last year. I thought it might be fun to work together again, that is all. Do you have many exciting cases?'

'Not in the slightest. Lost dogs, society scandals that need to be covered up, that sort of thing. But you surely do not intend to work at that bank for very long.'

'Perhaps. But I am doing very well. Now Miss Levine is being wasted there. All she is doing is typing stuff out of ledgers that doesn't need to be typed. As you were instrumental in getting us the work, I would be grateful if you could perhaps speak to Mr Drevey and point out to him that Miss Levine is not only an expert typist but that she has mastered Pitman shorthand.'

'I will see what I can do.'

After he had escorted Daisy and Rose back to their hostel and impressed on Miss Harringey the respectability of her tenants, Harry decided to go to the office. He found Miss Jubbles hard at work polishing his desk.

'Miss Jubbles! It is Sunday. What on earth are you doing here?'

Miss Jubbles blushed painfully. 'I was just passing and I thought I would do a few chores.'

'This will not do. You work too hard. Please go home.'

'I am sorry, Captain.'

She looked so upset that Harry said impulsively, 'I have been out on an odd case. Do you remember I told you I was doing some work for the Earl of Hadshire?'

'Yes, but you did not tell me exactly what was involved.'

So Harry told her the whole story. Miss Jubbles smiled, exclaimed, and listened intently while inside her brain a small, jealous Miss Jubbles was raging. That girl again. That wretched *beautiful* girl!

When he had finished telling her about Rose, Harry smiled and told Miss Jubbles to go home.

He gave her five shillings and told her to take a hack. Mrs Jubbles tore herself away. How sooty and cold and grim London looked! The hackney horse steamed and stamped as she climbed in and gave one last longing look up at the office windows.

The hack eventually dropped her at a thin, narrow brick house in Camden Town. Miss Jubbles lived with her widowed mother. She unlocked the front door and called, 'Mother!'

'In the sitting-room, dear' came a cry from upstairs.

Miss Jubbles mounted the narrow stairs to the first-floor sitting-room. Mrs Jubbles was sitting before a small coal fire which smouldered in the grate. She was a tiny woman dressed entirely in black. Her black lace cap hung over her withered features. Her black gown was trimmed with jet and her black-lace-mittened hands clutched a teacup.

When Miss Jubbles entered, she said in a surprisingly robust voice, 'Ring the bell for more tea, Dora.'

Miss Dora Jubbles pressed down the bell-push, and after a few minutes a small maid, breathless and with her cap askew, answered its summons. 'More tea, Elsie,' ordered Mrs Jubbles. 'And straighten your cap, girl.'

Mother and daughter exchanged sympathetic smiles after the girl had left. 'Servants,' sighed Mrs Jubbles as if used to a household of them rather than the overworked Elsie and a cross gin-soaked woman who came in the mornings to do the 'heavy work'.

'How did it go?' asked Mrs Jubbles eagerly.

Dora took off her coat and unpinned her large felt hat and stripped off her gloves. 'Wait until Elsie brings the tea-things. I've ever so much to tell you.'

From her daughter's tales, Mrs Jubbles had gathered that Captain Cathcart, younger son of a baron, who had chosen to sink to trade, was enamoured of her daughter. Both dreamt rosy dreams of being finally ensconced in some country mansion with a whole army of servants at their beck and call.

Elsie panted in with a tray with the tea-things and a plate containing two small Eccles cakes. Mother and daughter lived thriftily. Mrs Jubbles's husband had owned a butcher's shop in Camden Town and two houses other than the one the widow now lived in. She had sold all for a comfortable sum, but was keeping aside a substantial amount for her daughter's wedding. The fact that Dora was now thirty-eight years old had not dimmed her hopes. She saw Dora as elegant and distinguished.

Dora told her mother all about Lady Rose, ending with, 'She is very beautiful.'

Mrs Jubbles sniffed. 'You should tell the newspapers what this Lady Rose has been up to. They'd pay you and she'd be so socially ruined that he couldn't possibly want to marry her.'

Dora was shocked. 'I would be betraying the captain's trust. Oh, if you could have seen the way he smiled at me. There is an intimacy there, Mother, a warmth. And to confide in me the way he did? No, he seemed impatient with the adventures of this Lady Rose. He is never impatient with me.'

A little doubt crept into Mrs Jubbles mind. 'This Lady Rose is young?'

'Yes, very. Barely twenty, I would say.'

'And the captain is . . .?'

'Nearly thirty. Yes, he is younger than I am, but I think I am young-looking for my age.'

'Oh, yes, dear. Only the other day, the baker, Mr Jones said, "Where is your lovely daughter?" That's just what he said. So you do not think it would be a good idea to apprise the newspapers of what this Lady Rose is doing?'

'No, Mother. I would not breathe a word to anyone apart from you. And you must swear you must not tell anyone either.'

'There, there, girl. I swear,' said Mrs Jubbles and crossed her fingers behind her back.

Harry had forgotten to tell Mr Drevey about Daisy's prowess, the sick secretary had come back, and so Rose and Daisy were once more closeted together, typing out from the entries in the ledgers.

Rose was becoming weary of her new life. All her initial enthusiasm had gone, bit by bit. She longed to have a bed of her own again and decent meals. Her pin-money had gone quickly on items which Daisy had considered frivolous, such as an expensive vase for flowers and even more expensive flowers to put in it. Their wages had melted away on meals at Lyons, cosmetics, perfume that Rose felt she must have and new gloves and various other little luxuries. The winter weather was horrible.

The pin-money she had brought to her new life had run out and their combined wages did not allow them any luxuries. She was tired of cooking cheap meals on the gas ring in their room, tired of saving pennies for the gas meters, weary of the biting cold in this seemingly endless winter. She found that although Daisy did not like to read, she loved being read to, and so that was the way they passed most of their evenings.

Her clothes were beginning to smell of cooking, and regular sponging down with benzene did not seem to help much. Their underclothes had to be washed out in the bathroom and then hung on a rack before the gas fire. The sweat-pads from their blouses and dresses took ages to dry.

One morning Rose discovered a spot on her forehead. She could never remember having any spots on her face before.

She could only admire Daisy's fortitude. Daisy never complained. Rose did not know that Daisy, after her initial rush of gratitude after their escape, was as miserable as she was.

Daisy was every bit as conscious of the rigid English class distinctions as Rose and was afraid that any complaint from her would be treated as the typical whining of the lower classes.

One morning, as they arrived for work, it began to snow. Small little flakes at first and then great feathery ones already speckled with the dirty soot of London.

By lunchtime, it was a raging blizzard.

'We won't even be able to get along to Lyons for

lunch,' mourned Rose, 'and my back hurts with all this useless work.'

'There's a pie shop round the corner,' said Daisy.

'Oh, would you be a dear and get us something?' said Rose. 'I'll see if there is anywhere here I can make tea. I think there is a kitchen upstairs next to the executive offices. Take my umbrella.'

Daisy struggled out into the whirling snow. She bought two mutton pies and hurried back towards the office. A news-vendor was shouting, 'Society murder. Read all about it!'

Daisy bought a paper and breathed a sigh of relief when she entered the bank and shut the door on the white hell outside.

'I've got tea,' said Rose when she entered the room. 'There was no one upstairs. I'll wait until they have gone this evening and smuggle the tea things back. Mrs Danby won't see me. She never even comes near us any more, and Captain Cathcart must have forgotten that we wanted real work.'

'I've got the pies. Look at me coat,' said Daisy. 'Soaked already. We'll never get home in this.'

'Home,' echoed Rose bleakly, thinking of that awful room.

'Look, I bought the *Daily Mail*. There's something about a society murder. Here's your pie. You'll need to eat it out of the newspaper wrapping. No plates.'

Rose took a bite of the pie. 'This is really good. We should buy another two to take home.'

'I say!' exclaimed Daisy. 'You'll never believe who's gone and got himself murdered.'

'Who?'

'That Freddy Pomfret. Remember him? We met him at Telby Castle last year.'

'So we did,' said Rose.

'It says here, "Man-about-town, the Honourable Mr Frederick Pomfret, was found shot dead in his town flat in St James."'

As Daisy read on, Rose furrowed her brow. She remembered Freddy as vacuous and silly with his white face and patent leather hair. Hardly the man to incite anyone to murder him. But there was something else, something about Freddy nagging at the back of her mind.

At the end of the working day, they went out into a white world. London had gone to sleep under a thick blanket of snow.

'Let's see if the underground is working,' said Daisy. 'The Central London Railway goes to Holborn and then we can walk home.'

They stumbled through white drifts to King William Street Station and took the hydraulic lift down to the platforms. Trains consisted of three carriages hauled by electric locomotives. These were powered by the largest power-generating station in the country. The coaches were known as padded cells and they were long and narrow with high-backed cushioned seats and no windows. Gatemen stood on platforms at the end of each carriage to call out the names of the stations.

They paid the two pennies each fare and waited in the crush until they managed to get on 'the tube', as it was known.

'We should have travelled like this before,' said Rose. 'The omnibus is so slow. Why didn't we think about it?'

'I did,' said Daisy. 'But it frightens me to be so far underground with all them buildings on top of us.'

They got out at Holborn Station. The snow, which had eased a little when they left the office, had returned in all its ferocity. By the time they reached the hostel, they were cold and their clothes were soaked.

Rose searched in her purse. 'I have no pennies left. What about you?'

'No, but I've found a way to fix it.' Daisy crouched over the meter with an army knife bristling with gadgets and fiddled about with a thin blade until a penny rattled down and then another.

'Oh, Daisy, that's robbery.'

'That's warmth,' said Daisy cheerfully, dropping the coins back in, turning the dial and then lighting the small gas fire. They took off their wet clothes. Rose still felt self-conscious at disrobing in front of Daisy, but Daisy had no such qualms. She stripped naked and then wrapped herself in a wool dressing-gown and began to hang her clothes in front of the fire. Rose followed suit.

'Have we anything to eat?' she asked.

''Fraid not,' said Daisy gloomily.

There was a knock at the door. Rose opened it a crack. Miss Harringey stood there. 'A gentleman has called,' she said, her voice heavy with disapproval.

'Did he give a name?'

'A Mr Jarvis.'

'Tell him to wait and I will be down directly.'

Rose scrambled into dry clothes, leaving off the misery of stays, and hurried down the stairs.

Mr Jarvis stood in the hallway carrying a basket. 'Mr Jarvis! How on earth did you get here in this dreadful weather?' asked Rose.

'I rode one of the big horses, one of the ones that pull the fourgon. Here are some things for you' – he proffered the basket – 'and here is a letter. Please do not say anything. I think the lady of the house is listening. Good evening.'

He opened the street door and mounted the large shire-horse which was tethered outside, by dint of scraping snow off the low wall outside the house and using it as a mounting block.

Rose hurried upstairs. In the room, she opened the letter. It was from her mother, Lady Polly, to say that they had returned from Nice and would Rose please stop all this nonsense and come home.

'What's in the basket?' asked Daisy.

Rose lifted the cloth cover and gave a delighted cry. 'Food! Oh, do look, Daisy. Game pie and wine and biscuits, cake, tea, coffee, and he's even put in a bottle of milk. And there are other things.'

Daisy laid two plates and two cups on the table along with the cheap knives and forks they had purchased. 'We'll need to drink the wine out of teacups.'

'We haven't a corkscrew.'

'I have,' said Daisy, producing the knife again and twisting a corkscrew out from among the many implements.

As their clothes steamed and the room warmed up, both began to feel more cheerful. 'I know what it was,' said Rose suddenly.

'What?'

'About Freddy Pomfret. When I was working as secretary, one of the clerks came in and said, "Mr Pomfret has very generous friends." Mr Beveridge asked him what he meant and he said, "Three people have paid large deposits into his account so we don't need to send him any more letters about his overdraft."'

'Probably his relatives. But why didn't they pay up before? What you getting at?'

Rose was about to correct Daisy's grammar and remind her not to be so familiar but in time remembered that they were supposed to be on an equal footing.

'There must be some reason he was murdered. What if he was blackmailing people?'

Daisy looked doubtful. She thought it highly unlikely. The Freddy she remembered was silly but not villainous. Still, if Rose's detective urges had started up again, perhaps she would get in touch with Captain Cathcart. Daisy had a fondness for the captain's servant, Becket.

'We could ask Captain Cathcart.'

'Perhaps. I would like to see the books and then perhaps go to Scotland Yard and talk to Superintendent Kerridge.'

Daisy's face fell. 'Could we see the captain first?'

But Rose wanted to show the infuriating Harry that she could be a better detective than he was.

'I'll see what I can do tomorrow.'

'If we can even get to work,' Daisy pointed out.

The next morning was cold and still but the snow had stopped. As Rose and Daisy slipped and stumbled their way along to the underground station at Holborn, Rose wished she had packed her riding breeches. These long skirts and petticoats were useless attire for getting to work through a snowfall.

The City was quiet, shrouded in a blanket of snow. They had to knock at the bank door to gain admittance. At last one of the clerks opened the door to them.

'Nobody's turned up except me,' he said. 'I keep the door locked because anyone could walk in and rob the bank. Charles, the doorman, hasn't turned up and he's really got no excuse. He lives in the City. May I get you ladies anything? Tea?'

'Maybe later,' said Rose. 'We'll let you know. Thank you.'

Once they were in their office, Rose whispered, 'This is a perfect opportunity. I'll go upstairs to the counting-house and start searching.'

'What about the banking hall?'

'The records won't be there. In any case, everything in the banking hall will be tightly locked.'

Daisy lit the fire and then waited impatiently. Outside, she could hear the scraping of shovels and then the swish of brooms as the street-sweepers got to work. A shaft of sunlight suddenly shone down through the grimy window.

Then there came a banging at the front door. Daisy stayed where she was, nervously chewing at a thumbnail.

She heard the clerk running down the stairs. She stood up and opened the door of her office a crack. She heard the doorman complaining that he had a bad leg and it had taken him ages to struggle through the snow and then a female voice. Mrs Danby. Oh, where was Rose?

An hour passed. Daisy was just about to go out and up the stairs in case Rose was in trouble when the door opened and Rose slipped in.

'Where have you been?' hissed Daisy.

Rose sank down in her chair. 'It took me ages. But I've got some interesting information. Get on your coat and hat, Daisy. We're *going* to Scotland Yard. I telephoned Detective Superintendent Kerridge.'

'But what about old Danby?'

'We'll just need to risk her not knowing we even turned up for work.' They covered their typewriters and put on their coats, hats and gloves. Opening the door of their office, they crept out. To their relief, they could hear the doorman complaining about his leg to someone in the banking hall off to the left of the main door.

'Quickly,' said Rose.

CHAPTER FOUR

*Curs'd be the Bank of England notes, that tempt
a soul to sin.*

Sir Theodore Martin

Detective Superintendent Kerridge found he was looking forward to meeting Lady Rose again. After he had received her telephone call, he had in turn phoned Captain Cathcart. It pleased him to think they would all be together again, as they had been during that investigation the previous year at Telby Castle.

Kerridge was a grey man: grey hair, grey eyebrows, heavy grey moustache. He stood at the window of his office looking out at the Thames, and while he waited, he wrapped himself in one of his favourite dreams. In his mind he was a thinner, younger Kerridge manning the barricades at the People's Revolution of England. 'Down with the aristocrats!' he yelled and his supporters cheered. A beautiful young girl threw her arms around him and kissed him on the mouth. Kerridge blinked that part of the dream away. It was wrong to be unfaithful to his wife, even in dreams.

The door opened and Inspector Judd ushered Harry Cathcart in. 'What's this all about?' asked Harry.

'I received a telephone call from Lady Rose. She says she has vital information concerning the death of Freddy Pomfret.'

'I don't know how she could have come by any information about society at all in her present occupation.'

'Which is?'

'I'd better see if she wants to tell you.'

The door opened again. 'Lady Rose Summer and Miss Levine,' announced Judd.

'Your maid may wait outside,' said the detective, who had met Daisy before.

'Miss Levine is no longer my maid. She is my friend. She may stay.'

'Where's Becket?' asked Daisy.

'In Chelsea,' said Harry. Daisy's face fell.

'What are you doing here?' demanded Rose.

'I was summoned by Mr Kerridge,' said Harry, looking at Rose and thinking that a working life did not suit her. The hem of her coat was soaking from melted snow, her face was thinner and her eyes tired.

'Please sit down,' ordered Kerridge. 'Tea?'

'Oh, I would like tea,' said Rose, 'and perhaps some biscuits. We are very hungry.'

Kerridge picked up the phone and ordered tea, biscuits and cakes.

'Now, Lady Rose,' he said. 'Tell me what you have found out.

'Miss Levine and I have been working as typists at Drevey's Bank.'

'Why were you working as a typewriter?' asked Kerridge, who did not approve of new-fangled words like 'typist'.

'Because I wished to earn my living.'

'But you are taking employment away from some woman who really needs it,' said Kerridge.

'On the contrary. Captain Cathcart here arranged the work and it is make-work. Neither Miss Levine nor I are doing anything constructive. But if we could move on from your radical views, sir . . .'

'Go on.'

'For a short time I was working for a Mr Beveridge as his secretary. While I was in his office, one of the clerks came in and said something about large sums of money being deposited in Freddy Pomfret's account.

'Today, because of the snow, the bank was quiet, few having turned up to work. I went upstairs and searched until I found a statement of his account. During the last few months, three large sums of money were paid into that account. Each for ten thousand pounds.'

'Who gave him the money?'

'Lord Alfred Curtis, Mrs Angela Stockton, and Mrs Jerry Trumpington. I think,' said Rose triumphantly, 'that they were being blackmailed.'

'People lose a lot of money at cards,' Harry pointed out.

'Not for the same amount of money.'

'Lady Rose has a good point there,' said Kerridge, and Rose flashed Harry a triumphant look. 'His flat had been turned over, papers thrown everywhere, but his jewellery was left and fifty pounds in a desk drawer. So what do you know of those three?'

'I met Mrs Jerry last year, Mr Kerridge,' said Rose, 'and so did you. Large, gross sort of woman.'

'I remember.'

'I do not know Mrs Stockton or Lord Alfred.'

'I do,' said Harry. 'Mrs Stockton is a widow. She married an American millionaire who died soon after they were wed. Lord Alfred Curtis is a willowy young man. One of the lilies of the field.'

'The whole lot of them are lilies of the field,' grumbled Kerridge. 'A hard day's work would kill 'em.'

'Now, now, Mr Kerridge. You have before you three representatives of the working class and we are very much alive.'

'Sorry. I'll follow this up, Lady Rose. We shall ask all three why they paid him that particular sum of money.'

'You know,' said Harry, 'I bet all three say that Freddy was on his uppers and asked for that specific amount to clear his debts. If you like, I can start asking a few questions.'

'And I,' said Rose eagerly.

They were interrupted by the arrival of the tea-tray. Harry watched as Rose and Daisy enthusiastically munched their way through cakes and biscuits. 'You *are* hungry,' he said.

'We ate very well last night,' said Rose, 'but today we have had neither breakfast nor lunch because of the difficulty in getting to work through the snow and then in getting here. As I was saying, I can help further with the investigation.'

Harry suddenly saw a way of restoring Rose to her parents. 'You cannot do anything while you work at the bank – anything further, I mean. But were you to go back to your rightful position, you would be able to move freely in society again.'

'Good idea,' put in Daisy fervently, thinking of a blissful end to days of typewriting and evenings of cheap food.

'Yes, I suppose that would be a good idea,' said Rose, struck by a sudden vision of long hot baths and clean clothes.

'You have no objection, Mr Kerridge?'

'No, I shall be glad of any help. But do remember, Lady Rose, someone murdered Freddy Pomfret and will be prepared, no doubt, to murder again.'

'Then, Daisy, we will return to Eaton Square and tell the servants to collect our belongings, and Captain Cathcart can inform the bank that we will not be returning there.'

'I will certainly inform the bank on your behalf,' said Harry, 'but to send an earl's liveried servants to the hostel in Bloomsbury would occasion unwelcome comment. In the role as your brother, I will go back with you and find some form of transport to take you and your goods home.'

'What about your car?'

'Possible. They were spreading salt on the roads when I walked here. If I may use your telephone, I will ask Becket.'

Becket said that he thought he would be able to drive to Scotland Yard.

Harry could not help noticing that a sparkle had returned to Rose's blue eyes and correctly guessed that she was thrilled to have a suitable excuse to leave her working life and sordid hostel.

At the hostel, Miss Harringey began to complain that there would be no refund on the advance rent. Rose was about to declare haughtily that she could keep the money, but Harry sent her upstairs with Daisy to pack and then began to haggle. He did not want Miss Harringey to wonder too much about working women who could so easily forgo a refund.

At last he had to admit that he was defeated. Miss Harringey pointed out that she had no immediate hope of finding a new tenant for the room and therefore would be losing money.

Satisfied with her victory, she treated the captain to a glass of very inferior sherry.

Rose had wanted to leave all their clothes behind, but Daisy counselled her that such profligate behaviour would cause talk.

The carried their suitcases downstairs and Becket went up to collect the travelling trunk.

Outside, the sun had begun to shine and the snow was beginning to melt from the roofs.

Harry's car, with Becket at the wheel, conveyed them through the slippery melting roads to Eaton Square.

The hall-boy had seen them arrive and shouted the news. Two liveried footmen came down the front steps to carry in the luggage.

Then Brum, the butler, greeted them and said, 'I will inform my lord and my lady of your arrival.'

Rose had hoped to escape to her rooms, have a hot bath and a hair-wash and a change of clothes before either of her parents saw her, but as she and Daisy mounted the stairs, Rose's mother, Lady Polly, came out of the sitting-room on the first landing.

'Rose!' she exclaimed. 'Come in here immediately.'

The earl was asleep in front of the fire, a newspaper over his face.

'Wake up!' shouted Lady Polly. 'Rose is home!'

'Eh, what? By Jove, girl, you do look a mess. Sit down.'

Rose sank into a chair. Daisy remained standing, very much aware that she was a servant once again.

'What have you to say for yourself?' demanded Lady Polly.

'I am very grateful to you both for having allowed me to conduct the experiment of being a working woman,' said Rose. 'I feel I am now ready to return to society.'

'And what caused this sudden change of heart?'

'Daisy persuaded me it would be the proper thing to do.'

'Indeed!' Lady Polly smiled at Daisy for the first time. 'Well, well. I always said she was a sensible girl.'

'Yes, I am indebted to her.' Daisy wondered what had prompted Rose to give her credit for something she had not done.

'Are you sure nobody apart from Cathcart and Drevey knows of your escapade?' asked her father.

'No one else, Pa.'

'Very well,' said Lady Polly. 'Go of to your rooms and change. We will talk about your future later.'

At that moment, old Mrs Jubbles was talking about Rose to Mr Jones, the baker, who was seated in her drawing-room, balancing a cup of tea on one chubby knee.

'You see,' Mrs Jubbles was saying, 'it doesn't seem right she should get away with it. People like Lady Rose have no right to go out and work and take bread out of the mouths of those that need it. Also, I believe that Captain Cathcart may propose to my Dora and this Lady Rose is getting in the way. I would like to get rid of her.'

The teacup rattled nervously on the baker's knee. 'You don't mean . . .'

'No, silly. I mean I've a good mind to phone the *Daily Mail* and expose her. That way she'd be socially ruined and the captain wouldn't even look at her.'

Mr Jones was a round-shouldered greying man with small black eyes almost hidden in creases of fat. The delicate chair he was sitting on creaked alarmingly under his weight as he leaned forward. 'I don't think that would be a good idea,' he said, his sing-song voice betraying his Welsh origins.

Why? '

'Because this captain ain't in top society. I mean, he's put himself in trade. As it stands, Lady Rose's parents would never give their blessing. But if she was socially ruined, why then, she would be on a par with him.'

'I never thought of that. It's so good to have a man around to advise me. I do worry about Dora. I would like to see her married before I get married again myself.' She glanced roguishly at the baker.

'As to that,' said Mr Jones, turning red, 'I have a proposition to make.'

Mrs Jubbles put one thin old hand up to her bosom. 'Oh, Mr Jones!'

'Yes. See, I've a mind to ask Dora myself.'

'Dora!' screeched Mrs Jubbles. 'My Dora! Her what's meant for the captain. Get out of here and don't come back.'

Mr Jones stood up and laid his teacup down on a side table which had just been beyond his reach.

'I was only trying to help,' he said huffily.

Mrs Jubbles raised her trembling black-lace-mittened hands and shouted, 'Out! Out! Out!'

And so Mr Jones left, bewildered, not knowing that Mrs Jubbles had believed his visits were because he was enamoured of *her*.

Madly, she blamed this Lady Rose. Things had been going so well before *she* appeared on the scene.

Harry decided to call on Lord Alfred Curtis to start his investigations. Lord Alfred lived in a house in Eaton Terrace. His manservant answered the door and took Harry's card. He studied it and then ushered Harry into one of those ante-rooms off the front hall reserved for tradesmen and other hoi polloi.

Harry reflected ruefully that even society's servants knew he had sunk to trade.

He waited and waited. At last the door opened and Lord Alfred swanned in, wrapped in a brightly coloured oriental dressing-gown. 'You woke me,' he said by way of greeting, but Harry noticed that the young man had shaved and that his thick brown hair was smarmed down with Macassar oil. Lord Alfred yawned and said, 'What's this about?'

'It's about the death of Freddy Pomfret.'

Alfred composed his thin face and heavy-lidded eyes into what he obviously considered was the correct mask of mourning. 'Poor fellow. Commit suicide, did he?'

'No, he was shot.'

'Terribly, frightfully, awfully sad. So what's it got to do with me?'

'You paid him ten thousand pounds.'

'So? I must sit down. I'm getting a sore neck with you looming over me. Let's go into the morning-room.'

Harry followed him up the stairs and into a room off the first landing. It was decorated in gold: gold-embossed paper on the wall, gold silk furniture, gold carpet.

There was a fire crackling in the grate. 'Sit down,' ordered Alfred with a wave of one long white hand.

They both sat down opposite each other.

'I was asking you why you gave Freddy ten thousand pounds. I'm acting on behalf of his family,' lied Harry.

'Let me think.' Alfred placed the tip of one finger against his brow, rather in the manner of the Dodo in

Alice's Adventures in Wonderland. 'Ah, yes, he was on his uppers. Begged a loan to pay off his gambling debts.'

'Do you have an IOU?'

'Of course not. Gentleman's agreement. You wouldn't understand.' His voice held the hint of a sneer.

'No, I don't,' said Harry bluntly. 'It's the first time I've ever heard of anyone in society lending that amount of money without first securing a note.'

'Really? I have heard you don't get about so much in the world these days.' The 'world' to Alfred meant the world of society. After all, for him, no other world existed.

'He wasn't blackmailing you, was he?'

Lord Alfred rang the bell beside the fireplace and stood up. 'You are leaving now. Don't ever come here again with your nasty remarks. Ah, Gerhardt, show this person out.'

The manservant, a powerfully built man, advanced on Harry.

'I'm leaving,' said Harry, 'but you will be hearing from me again.'

Alfred sank back in his chair. 'Go away,' he said. 'Never come near me again.'

Rose lay in a scented bath and wondered what to do about Daisy. Because they had been equals when they were working, the fact that Daisy was once more her servant made Rose feel uncomfortable. She had put herself down to Daisy's level. Perhaps there would be some way to bring Daisy up nearer her own.

After the maids had dried her, Rose dismissed them. She decided to dress herself, but realized that she would need help with her stays and rang the bell.

'Sorry, my lady,' said Daisy, looking flustered. 'I should have been with you earlier.'

'Help me with my stays, Daisy. The problem is that I can no longer look on you as a servant.'

'Do you want to get rid of me?' asked Daisy in a small voice.

'After all we have been through together! Of course not. What am I to wear?'

Daisy glanced at the clock. 'The tea-gown with the lace panels, I think. It's still quite cold, so you'd better take your Paisley shawl.'

When she was dressed and her hair had been put up, Rose said, 'There is no need for you to be on duty in the drawing-room. I wish to speak to my parents in private.'

Harry rang the doorbell of Mrs Jerry Trumpington's home. He hoped he would have more success with her than he had had with Lord Alfred. He handed his card, and after a few moments was ushered into Mrs Jerry's sitting-room. She was a vast toad-like woman who carried little bits of food about her dress as a testimony to her gluttony. She had eaten quail for luncheon, Harry noticed, identifying a small bone in the black lace on Mrs Jerry's bosom, followed by, possibly, Dover sole – there were fish bones, also – and, he guessed, in a mornay sauce, the sauce having caused a thin yellow edge on the lace.

'Why, my very dear Captain,' she said, her thick lips opening in a smile. 'How goes the world?'

'Very baffling,' said Harry, sitting down opposite her.

'I was about to take tea. Will you join me?'

'Too kind.'

Mrs Jerry rang the bell and ordered tea for two.

'The reason I am here,' said Harry, 'is because of the death of Freddy Pomfret.'

'Poor chap.'

'Indeed. Why did you pay Freddy ten thousand pounds?'

She sat very still, her slightly bulbous eyes fixed on his face. Then she said, 'Did I?'

'Yes.'

'Oh, I remember. He was short of the ready, that's all. I'm a generous soul.'

'Ten thousand pounds would be considered a fortune to most people in this country.'

'But I am not most people. How did you find out?'

'I heard something at Scotland Yard. No doubt the police have been in touch with his bank.' Harry could imagine Mrs Jerry's fury if she knew the real source of the information.

Two footmen came in carrying the tea-things. Mrs Jerry waited until they had both been served and then waved the servants away. When the door had closed behind them, she said, 'What's it got to do with you, anyway?'

'I am working for his family,' said Harry, feeling that he really must contact Freddy's family as soon as possible before he was caught out in his lies.

'I really think the – er – trade you are in is most distasteful.' Mrs Jerry ignored the thin bread and butter and the mounds of sandwiches and fruitcakes and selected a meringue filled with cream.

'Was Freddy blackmailing you?' asked Harry.

She bit down on the meringue so violently that a shower of meringue crumbs, meringue powder, and a dollop of cream joined the detritus of food on her bosom.

'Geffout!' she roared when she could.

'I beg your pardon?'

She seized a napkin and wiped her mouth. She lumbered to her feet, panting with rage.

'Out!' she shouted. 'And never darken my doorstep again.'

'I didn't know anyone actually said that apart from the stage,' said Harry equably. 'If Freddy was not blackmailing you, why are you so furious?'

Mrs Freddy rang the bell. 'Because of your impertinence. Because I am a respectable woman without a stain on my character.'

'Unlike your dress, madam? You are covered in food. You are a walking menu.'

The footmen entered. 'Throw him out!' howled Mrs Jerry, collapsing back in her chair.

'It's all right, I'm going,' said Harry.

As he walked outside, he wondered if he had been too blunt. He reflected ruefully that he would not be able to contact Rose because he had nothing to tell her, and in the same moment wondered why that should matter so much.

* * *

'So pleasant to see you looking your old self again,' sighed Lady Polly. 'We have decided to launch you back into society by gentle degrees.'

To her mother's surprise, Rose did not object but merely lowered her long eyelashes and said meekly, 'Yes, indeed.'

'There are various cards here. We will go through them and decide which ones to accept.'

Rose's sharp eyes caught sight of a name – Mrs Angela Stockton. She picked up the card. Mrs Angela Stockton was requesting the pleasure of the earl and countess and their daughter at a lecture she was giving on Rudolf Steiner.

'This looks interesting.'

The countess raised her lorgnette and studied the card. 'It's for tomorrow afternoon. Too late to accept now. Besides, who is Rudolf Steiner?'

'It would be interesting to find out.'

'I have no intention of going, even although the woman is perfectly respectable.'

'I would like to go – with Daisy.'

'As to Daisy,' said Lady Polly, 'I fear you may have become over-familiar with her.'

'I agree. So I am going to make her my companion and hire a lady's maid.'

'Out of the question.'

'It was Daisy who persuaded me to leave my working life. You are always worried that I will do something disgraceful. Daisy takes care of me. Why, she was even shocked that I should threaten to tell society how you arranged for the road and railway station at Stacey Court to be blown up so that the king would not visit us.'

'Quite right. I hope you have dropped that silly nonsense.'

'I'll need to think about it. Of course, were Daisy elevated to my companion, I wouldn't dream of mentioning it.'

'We spoilt you,' said Lady Polly bitterly. 'Most young gels who behaved the way you have behaved would have been locked up in the asylum by now. Wake up!' she suddenly shouted at her husband.

'Hey, what!' The little earl blinked like an owl.

'Tea is served and your daughter wants to make that maid of hers a companion.'

'And what does Cathcart have to say about that?'

'Cathcart! He has nothing to say in what our daughter does or does not do.'

'You must admit he saved her bacon on more than one occasion.' The earl rang the bell and when the butler answered it, he said, 'Brum, fetch the telephone.'

'My lord, that instrument does not detach from the study. It is necessary for one to go to the machine.'

'Well, go to it and phone that Cathcart fellow and tell him to come here.'

'It would be better to send a carriage for him,' said Rose quickly, fearing that Miss Jubbles would take the call and not pass it on. 'His office is in the Buckingham Palace Road. Number Twenty-five-A.'

'Very well, jump to it,' said the earl. 'By Jove, do I see Madeira cake?'

* * *

73

Looking down from the window, Miss Jubbles saw the carriage with the crest on the panels drawing up outside and a liveried footman jumping down from the backstrap.

She heard footsteps on the stairs. The footman entered. 'I am here to take Captain Cathcart to visit the Earl of Hadshire.'

Miss Jubbles's heart beat hard. That girl again!

'I am afraid,' she announced in tones of stultifying gentility, 'that Captain Cathcart is not here. He has gone abroad.'

'And when is he expected back?'

'He did not say.'

'When he returns, tell him to contact his lordship immediately.'

'Certainly.'

And then Miss Jubbles heard that familiar tread on the stairs. Harry had suffered a shrapnel wound during the Boer War, and on the bad days, walked with a pronounced limp, and this was one of the bad days.

He entered the office and paused in the doorway. He had recognized the earl's carriage outside.

'Captain Cathcart,' cried the footman, who recognized Harry from his visits to the earl's home. 'Your secretary said you had gone abroad.'

Miss Jubbles's face was red with mortification. 'I am sorry, sir,' she said. 'When I said abroad, I meant abroad in London.'

'That's all right,' said Harry. 'But the earl is a client and an important one. You knew I was due back here late afternoon because I told you.'

'I am so sorry. I forgot.' And with that, Miss Jubbles burst into tears.

'Don't take on so,' said Harry. 'I have to pick up some papers from my desk. There's nothing else for you to do this afternoon.'

He went through to his office. On his desk was a small vase of freesias, imported from the Channel Islands. He scowled down at them. They were expensive. He took some papers off his desk and walked out.

'Miss Jubbles,' he said gently, 'I appreciate the flowers but they are much too expensive a gift. Please extract the amount from petty cash.'

'Oh, sir, they were only a little present.'

'Please do as you are told,' ordered Harry, 'and enter the amount in the petty-cash book.'

Tears rolled down Miss Jubbles's cheeks. 'Here,' said Harry, handing her a large handkerchief. 'Now, I must go.'

He was beginning to suspect that his secretary's feelings for him might be a trifle too warm, but never for a moment did Harry guess at the depth of the obsession that would cause her to sleep with the handkerchief against her cheek that night.

Harry turned in the doorway. 'And do not accept any more cases. I am going to be tied up with one important one for the foreseeable future.'

'Come in, Cathcart,' cried the earl. 'Tea?'

'No, thank you. Do you have a problem?'

Rose had been sent to her room.

'It's Rose again. She wants to make that Cockney maid of hers a companion. She does give Daisy the credit, I gather, for having persuaded her to get back in society.'

'I think it might be a very good idea,' said Harry. 'Daisy's demeanour is suitable, and with the right clothes she would not occasion comment.'

'But companions have *background*!'

'Then give her one. Any respectable recluse you know of in Hadshire who died recently?'

'Well, let me see. There was Sir Percy Anstruther.'

'Married?'

'Married a girl half his age, who ran off and left him.'

'Any surviving family?'

'None as far as I know. I think the estate went to the Crown.'

'Good. Daisy is his long-lost daughter. She fell on hard times. Her mother had reverted to her maiden name of Levine. You rescued her. All respectable. You discovered her true identity after she had been working as your daughter's maid and promptly elevated her to companion in respect for your old friend, Sir Percy. She is a strong, moral girl and will keep a guard of Lady Rose.'

'I sometimes think,' put in Lady Polly, 'that it might be an idea to give Rose just a taste of the asylum to discipline her.'

'But think of the scandal,' said Harry. 'She would be lost to you and damned as mad for the rest of her life.'

'Oh, very well,' said Lady Polly. 'But I will hire a lady's maid for her and one that will keep a strict eye on her as well. Rose has some very odd ideas about going into society again. She insists on going to some boring lecture given by Mrs Angela Stockton.'

'Mrs Stockton,' said Harry, consulting the papers he had taken from his office, 'is fabulously wealthy and of good family.'

'But a lecture . . . !'

'And has a son of Rose's age.'

Both the earl and countess looked at Harry. 'Now that's different,' said the earl. 'Nothing up with money in the family, hey.'

CHAPTER FIVE

I am silent in the Club,
I am silent in the pub,
I am silent on a bally peak in Darien;
For I stuff away for life
Shoving peas in with a knife,
Because I am at heart a Vegetarian.

No more the milk of cows
Shall pollute my private house
Than the milk of the wild mares of the Barbarian:
I will stick to port and sherry,
For they are so very, very,
So very, very, very Vegetarian

G. K. Chesterton

The fact that the earl and countess agreed to their daughter's attending Angela Stockton's lecture accompanied only by her new companion was prompted by parental weariness. Where had they gone wrong? They had supplied her with the best governess – or so they had believed – and the fact that they saw very little of her until she became of an age to be a débutante could not surely have created any problem, for she had been brought up as a lady of her class.

They had enjoyed their visit to Nice, the long miles separating them from their unruly daughter having largely served to put Rose out of their minds. Angela Stockton's lecture seemed a safe enough place for her to be seen. Also, there was the carrot of Mrs Stockton's marriageable son.

Luncheon was to be served before the lecture. Mrs Stockton's impressive home was in Knightsbridge. Daisy, self-conscious in her new grand clothes supplied from Rose's wardrobe, felt she would have enjoyed the outing better had not Lady Polly sent her lady's maid, Humphrey, to keep an eye on them. Daisy was conscious the whole time of Humphrey's hot and jealous eyes.

A fork luncheon was served in a long dining-room. The other guests were women of indeterminate age, some of them wearing very odd clothes, consisting of cotton embellished with cabalistic designs. There were a few men, mostly reedy and starved-looking.

Mrs Angela Stockton greeted them warmly. She was dressed in black velvet with stars and moons embroidered in silver around the hem of her gown. A heavy silver belt was around her waist and silver necklaces jangled from her thin neck. She had hair of an improbable shade of red, piled up and held in place with what looked like two ivory chopsticks. Her heavily rouged mouth was surrounded by a radius of wrinkles. Her eyes, outlined in kohl, were very large and pale blue.

'I am flattered that one so young and ~~beautiful~~ should grace my humble home,' she said. 'May I introduce my son, Peregrine.'

Daisy reflected that Peregrine looked like a stage-door Johnny. He had thick black hair, well-oiled, and a thick luxuriant black moustache. His waistcoat was a violent affair of red and gold silk.

Rose and Daisy moved on into the dining-room. 'Rabbit food,' hissed Daisy.

They helped themselves to nut cutlets and salad. There was no wine, simply jugs of water.

Daisy and Rose sat down at a table. 'It's quite tasty but they might at least have served the nut cutlets hot,' complained Rose. 'And this house is abominably cold.' She signalled to Humphrey and asked her to fetch her fur coat from the ante-room where they had left their outer wrappings. 'Miss Levine's coat as well.'

Humphrey glared at Daisy and then went off, returning shortly with their coats.

'That's better,' said Rose. 'I think we should hear what the lecture is about and then talk to Mrs Stockton afterwards. We cannot ask her outright about the ten thousand pounds or she will ask how we came by our information. But we can get to know her and find out if there is anything about her, any weakness, that would cause her to be blackmailed.'

'You could get close to that son of hers easily enough,' said Daisy. 'He's leering at you across the room.'

'I don't think I could bear it.' Rose speared a lettuce leaf and looked at it gloomily. 'I am going to be quite hungry after this. Did you see any bread?'

'Not a bit.'

'Then it's more nut cutlets, I'm afraid. Oh, look, they are serving coffee and tea at that other table.'

They helped themselves to more cutlets, but found that the tea was camomile and the coffee, dandelion.

'I'm sure it's all very healthy,' mourned Daisy. 'What I'd give for a pint of beer and a meat pie.'

At last they were summoned to the lecture, which was to take place in a drawing-room on the first floor.

'Who is Rudolf Steiner anyway?' asked Daisy as they took their seats.

'I asked Jarvis this morning. Pa's secretary is a fund of knowledge. He said that Steiner is an occult philosopher.'

'Occult? Witches and warlocks?'

'No, something to do with the world of the spirit.'

Mrs Stockton stood on a stage which had been erected at the end of the room. 'My lord, ladies and gentlemen,' she began. 'As you know, like Mr Steiner, we are all dedicated vegetarians. Meat corrupts the body and banishes us from the world of the spirit.

'As our great teacher said, "The soul which gives itself over to the inner illumination recognizes in itself not only what it was *before* the illumination; it also recognizes what it has become only *through* this illumination."'

'What does that mean?' whispered Daisy.

'Blessed if I know,' said Rose, burrowing deeper into her furs.

Despite the warmth provided by the fur coat given to her by Rose, Daisy could feel the tip of her nose turning pink and her feet were like two blocks of ice.

Mrs Stockton's words drifted in and out of her brain. '"No one is hindered from making fruitful in the natural and social realms that which is brought over from the wellspring of spiritual life by those who have the right to speak of the principle of initiation," so speaks the master.'

Then Daisy began to become uneasily aware of gas building up under her stays. She realized she would need to get out of the room before she delivered herself of what her family in the East End would call a 'real knicker ripper'.

She murmured an excuse and edged out of the room, trying to walk and keep her buttocks firmly clenched at the same time.

Daisy went down the stairs and stood in the hall, but before she could relieve herself of gas, an arm went round her waist and a voice in her ear said, 'Looking for me, my pretty?'

She swung round and found Peregrine Stockton smiling down at her and twisting his moustache like a stage villain.

'I needed some air,' said Daisy. Her eyes, which were green and slightly prominent, felt as if they would burst from their sockets and roll across the floor like two marbles.

'What about a kiss for a poor chap?'

He tried to slide his arm around her waist again, but Daisy backed off and then exploded. A loud sound like a raspberry echoed around the hall and Daisy stood there with her face flaming.

'Hem, well, jolly cold day, what,' he said, backing away. 'Get back to hear Mother's lecture, what.'

He darted off up the stairs. Daisy was scarlet with mortification. Her first day out as a companion in all her grand clothes and she had disgraced herself. She trailed miserably back up the stairs. But the first thing that struck her when she entered the drawing-room was that she was far from being the only sufferer. The effect of nut cutlets and raw vegetables on so many middle-aged and elderly digestive systems was taking its toll.

She joined Rose, who was sitting with a scented handkerchief pressed to her nose.

'There's an awful smell in here. What is it?' whispered Rose.

'Essence of fart,' whispered Daisy. 'It was them nut cutlets.'

'Daisy, you must not use these crude Anglo-Saxon words.'

'What should I have said?'

'Shhh, I'll tell you afterwards.'

Mrs Stockton was now lecturing her audience on the benefits of vegetarianism. Then she asked for questions. One middle-aged man who looked fit and healthy, certainly compared with the others about him, rose to his feet. 'I am a vegetarian,' he said. 'But I think people should be told that there are many attractive and *hot* vegetarian dishes which are just as good as meat. Eating too many raw vegetables can be upsetting to the stomach.' A sudden volley like gunshot from the ladies behind him interrupted his speech. Daisy emulated Rose, and pressed a handkerchief to her nose. The gentleman tried to go on, but his face suddenly creased up with laughter. He tried to control himself but a great guffaw burst from his lips.

'The lecture is finished,' shouted Mrs Stockton. There was a polite smattering of applause.

Mrs Stockton then positioned herself at the door of the drawing-room to say goodbye to her guests.

Rose shook her hand and said, 'I wonder if I might consult you. I am very interested in vegetarianism.'

'Indeed?' Mrs Stockton gave a gratified smile. 'If you would care to wait until I say goodbye to everyone, then we can have a cosy chat.'

Rose and Daisy retreated back into the drawing-room. At last Mrs Stockton begged them to follow her to her study.

'You may wait here for us, Humphrey,' ordered Rose.

Mrs Stockton led them across the landing and into a room where the walls were draped in black velvet and a scented candle burnt on a table, also draped in black.

'Now, where shall I begin?' she began brightly.

A butler entered with a card on a tray. 'A Captain Cathcart to see you, madam.'

'You must tell him I am otherwise engaged.'

'The gentleman said it would only take a few minutes.'

'What can he want? Oh, do show him up.' She smiled at Rose. 'Another of my admirers, no doubt, but I confess I cannot quite place the name.'

'Captain Cathcart,' said Rose, 'is a private investigator.'

'Oh dear, how common. I must get rid of him

immediately.' She reached out to ring the bell, but at that moment Harry was ushered into the room.

'I should not have allowed you to come up,' said Mrs Stockton. 'I do not entertain *persons*.'

'Just one question,' said Harry. 'Good afternoon, Lady Rose, Miss Levine. Mrs Stockton, was Mr Pomfret blackmailing you?'

'Who, pray, is Mr Pomfret?'

'The young man who has just been murdered. The young man to whom you gave ten thousand pounds.'

Rose studied Mrs Stockton's face. It had become almost mask-like. 'Ah, yes, I remember now. He was interested in setting up a series of lectures on vegetarianism. A worthy cause. I always support worthy causes.'

'Mr Pomfret was a loyal member of the Beefsteak Club. They hold dinners every month and a great quantity of beef is eaten.'

'Then he must have reformed. Please leave. Lady Rose, you must forgive me, but my exertions this afternoon have given me the headache. Perhaps another time?'

'Certainly,' said Rose. 'Would tomorrow afternoon be convenient?'

'I should be honoured. Shall we say three o'clock? Yes? Good. Now, if you will excuse me. Captain Cathcart, do not come here again.'

'Let's go to my office and discuss what we have,' said Harry as they walked down the stairs.

'I'd best get rid of Humphrey,' said Rose. 'We'll never get any privacy with her around. She disapproves of Daisy and she is jealous.'

* * *

Miss Jubbles surveyed the arrivals with gloom. 'Tea, please, Miss Jubbles,' said Harry pleasantly as he ushered Daisy and Rose into the inner office.

Miss Jubbles felt a lump in her throat as she opened a cupboard and took out the pretty cups and saucers reserved for guests. She went out into the corridor and into the toilet, where she filled the kettle at the sink. Once back in the office, she pulled out the gas ring by the fire, lit it, and placed the kettle on it.

She arranged three cups on a tray, then milk and sugar and a plate of Abernethy biscuits. The kettle boiled. She put tea-leaves into a fat yellow china teapot. Miss Jubbles stared at the tray. Sugar tongs. She had forgotten the sugar tongs. She went back to the cupboard and her eye fell on a packet of powdered senna pods. Miss Jubbles suffered from constipation. All at once she thought she saw a way of getting rid of these unwanted guests.

She poured three cups of tea, but to two of the cups she added a spoonful of the senna powder.

Miss Jubbles carried the tray in. She carefully placed the two already poured cups in front of Daisy and Rose and then poured a cup for Harry.

'Thank you, Miss Jubbles,' said Harry. 'That will be all.'

Miss Jubbles retreated.

Rose raised her hand to pick up a cup, but Daisy said, 'Don't drink it.'

'Why?' asked Rose.

'There's some sort of powder floating in it. I bet that Jubbles female put something in our tea.'

'Come now,' said Harry. 'This is not the theatre. She would not dare.'

'Then get *her* to drink it.'

Harry looked amused. 'Very well, Daisy. If it will put your silly fears at rest.'

'You can't call her Daisy anymore,' protested Rose. 'Now she is my companion, you must address her as Miss Levine.'

Harry went to the door and opened it. 'Miss Jubbles, would you step in here for a moment?'

Miss Jubbles came in and stood there meekly, her hands folded.

'Miss Jubbles,' said Harry, picking up Rose's cup. 'Please drink this.'

'I r-really d-don't feel l-like drinking tea at the moment,' stammered Miss Jubbles.

'It's simply to put Miss Levine's fears at rest. She thinks there is something in the tea.'

'Why, that is ridiculous,' said Miss Jubbles, turning red. 'I'll show you.' She picked up the cup of tea and drank it down.

'There!' she panted.

'You see, Miss Levine?' said Harry. 'I think an apology is in order.'

'I am very sorry,' said Daisy.

'You may go, Miss Jubbles.'

Miss Jubbles retreated to her room and sat there miserably. She had already taken senna powder that morning and knew that this added dose would have dire results.

'Now, where were we?' said Harry.

'Discussing possible blackmail,' said Rose. 'I think perhaps you went about it the wrong way.'

'What makes you say that?'

'To bluntly ask Mrs Stockton whether she was being blackmailed puts her on her guard.'

'And how would you have gone about it?'

'I have started,' said Rose. 'I shall befriend Mrs Stockton. I shall get close to her. In order to find out why she was being blackmailed, I have to understand her better.'

'Very well. For my part,' said Harry, 'I must visit Freddy's parents and see if they are prepared to employ me.'

'Who are his parents?' asked Daisy.

'A certain Colonel and Mrs Pomfret. I believe they are in town. They have a town house in Kensington.'

'What about Detective Superintendent Kerridge?'

'I phoned him with my lack of success with Mrs Jerry and Lord Alfred and he said in that weary way of his that he should never have left it to amateurs and that he would see them himself.'

Kerridge had had every intention of interviewing the suspects. It was his job. But he admitted to himself that he'd been cowardly in letting Captain Cathcart go first.

Accompanied by Detective Inspector Judd, he set out to interview Lord Alfred Curtis. At least he knew that the young lord was expecting him. His secretary had made an appointment.

The gas lamps had already been lit and a thin drizzle was falling as he was driven in the new police car to Lord Alfred's residence.

He climbed down from the car with great reluctance. He detested interviewing the aristocracy.

To his surprise and relief, he was warmly welcomed. Lord Alfred rose to his feet and advanced on him with hand outstretched when Kerridge was ushered into a pretty drawing-room.

'Do sit down, Mr Kerridge,' said Lord Alfred. 'Miserable evening, what? May I offer you something?'

'Nothing, I thank you,' said Kerridge. 'Do you know why I am here?'

'It's something to do with poor Freddy's death, is it not? I had that peculiar Captain Cathcart here earlier accusing me of being blackmailed by Freddy. Ridiculous! When a gentleman sinks to trade, it alters his very brain. Sees common little plots and conspiracies everywhere.'

'We have ascertained that three people each paid Mr Pomfret the sum of ten thousand pounds. We did think it might be a case of blackmail.'

'Well, now I've calmed down, I can see why you might jump to that conclusion. But the man was on his uppers. Some people will gamble ferociously when they haven't got the ready. Poor, poor Freddy. I never even thought to ask for an IOU, so it's not as if I can even claim on his estate. Who are the other two?'

'At this stage of the investigation, I would prefer not

to say, my lord. Now, do you know of any enemies Mr Pomfret might have had?'

'The trouble is, one didn't know him very *well*. There are a great number of people in the world one doesn't know very well.'

'And yet you lent him a vast sum of money.'

'To tell the truth, I had drunk a little more than was good for me. It's all coming back to me. It was in The Club. Everything was a bit jolly, and so when Freddy sprang the request on me, I gave him a cheque, almost without thinking. The claret at The Club is very good, but it does produce a dangerous feeling of euphoria. I was quite convinced at that time that he must be one of my dearest friends.'

'And Mr Pomfret specifically asked for ten thousand pounds?'

'Oh, yes, just like that. Tristram Baker-Willis was there at the time. He did protest, you know. "I say, Freddy, that's a bit steep." Those were his very words.'

'Ah. Where can I find Mr Baker-Willis?'

'At this time, he'll be at his diggings in Pall Mall, getting ready for the evening ahead.' He gave the detective superintendent the number in Pall Mall.

'I think that will be all for the moment,' said Kerridge, rising to his feet.

Tristram Baker-Willis was just as Kerridge remembered him. He had met the young man the previous year during investigations at Telby Castle. Tristram had a very white face, thick lips and black hair greased to a high shine. His waistcoat was a riot of brightly embroidered silk flowers.

'We have just been paying Lord Alfred Curtis a visit,' began Kerridge. 'Judd, what did he say?'

The detective opened his notebook, flicked the pages and then repeated what Lord Alfred had said about Tristram being present when Freddy had asked for that loan.

'Yes, that's right,' said Tristram. 'Anything else?'

'Yes, of course. Do you mean that Mr Pomfret went straight up to Lord Alfred and said, "Lend me ten thousand pounds?"'

'Yes, something like that. I said, "Hey, Freddy! What are you doing?" Lord Alfred had taken drink. He wrote out that cheque with such a shaky hand, I thought Freddy would never be able to cash it.'

'Well, he did. Mr Pomfret was also paid ten thousand pounds by two other people.'

'Good heavens! Good old Freddy. Wish I had his talent for getting money out of people. Do you mean two other people paid him ten thousand *each*?'

'That is so. Do you know if it is possible that Mr Pomfret was indulging in blackmail?'

'Hey, he was a friend of mine. Stout fellow. Wouldn't harm a fly.' Tristram leaned forward and said earnestly, 'Look here, Inspector . . .'

'Superintendent.'

'Superintendent. You usually deal with the lower classes and it has given you a warped view of life. Such as we do not go around blackmailing people.'

'Had Mr Pomfret any enemies?'

'No, everybody liked Freddy. I liked Freddy. Best friend I ever had.' Tristram took a handkerchief out of his sleeve and blew his nose loudly.

'So,' said Kerridge heavily, 'my inspector has a note of your evidence. I gather you would be prepared to stand up in court, kiss the Bible, and say the same thing?'

'Court! It'll never come to court.'

'Why not? It's murder and I intend to find the murderer.'

Tristram kneaded the handkerchief between his fingers and scowled at the floor. Then his face cleared. 'Ah, but only if Alfred is the murderer, and that is ridiculous.'

'That will be all for now,' said Kerridge. 'If you would be so good as to call at Scotland Yard tomorrow, we will take your statement, type it up, and you may sign it.'

Tristram looked to right and left as if seeking a way out. 'Can't,' he said finally. 'Going to the country tomorrow.'

'Then I suggest you come with us now.'

'No, I won't,' said Tristram. 'I must warn you that I have friends at the Palace.'

'Mr Baker-Willis, unless you are prepared to make an official statement, I must assume you are lying.'

Tristram stared at him for a long moment. Then he shrugged. 'May as well get it over with. I'll come now.'

Later that evening, armed with a letter of introduction from an old army friend, Brigadier Bill Handy, Harry visited the late Freddy's father. Colonel Hugh Pomfret read the letter carefully. Then he said, 'Of course I want to find out who murdered my son. But what can you do that the police cannot?'

'I have more freedom to go about in society than the police and to find out what enemies your son had.'

'Very well. Go ahead.' Then, with a slight edge of contempt in his voice. 'I suppose you want paid for your services.'

'No, because I came to you and not the other way round.'

'Very good of you,' said the colonel gruffly.

'Did your son keep any letters or correspondence with you?'

'No, the only time he came here was to ask for money, and when he got it or didn't get it, he would leave. He came to the family place in the country at Christmas. Apart from that, we barely saw him.

'My wife is distraught. Like all mothers, she remembers him as a small boy now, but truth to tell, our son had become a nasty, jeering sort of person whenever we saw him. He didn't like the fact that I haven't a title. He hung around the fringes of the Kensington Palace set. He wanted me to *buy* him a title. That was in January. When I told him I had not that kind of money and if I had I would not spend it on such rubbish, he stormed out.'

So that's what he wanted the money for, thought Harry. Who would have thought that such a light-weight young man could be so ferociously ambitious?

* * *

'So you let them send you away?' Lady Polly demanded of the quaking Humphrey.

'I couldn't do otherwise, my lady. It's my nerves.'

'You know, Humphrey, I am tired of those nerves of yours. Mrs Cummings was telling me that there is a very good nerve doctor.' She rummaged in a capacious reticule and found a small notebook and flicked it open.

'Here we are. Dr Thomas McWhirter. He's in Harley Street. Get Jarvis to phone and make an appointment for you and then perhaps we'll hear less about your nerves.'

Lady Polly felt quite noble. She believed in looking after her servants. She did not know that she was setting in train a course of events that would put Rose in danger.

The following afternoon, Rose and Daisy visited Angela Stockton. Rose was disappointed to find Mrs Stockton's son, Peregrine, there as well. Fennel tea was served and some jaw-breaking biscuits.

'I found your lecture very interesting,' said Rose, averting her eyes from Peregrine, whose hot gaze was fastened on her face.

'Oh, go on with you,' laughed Peregrine. 'Pretty creature like you. Got better to do with your time, hey?'

Angela put down her cup with an angry little click. 'Peregrine, I wish to talk to these ladies alone.'

'I'll tootle off, then. Don't know how you can drink that muck.'

Peregrine left the room and Rose heaved a sigh of relief. 'You must forgive Perry,' sighed Angela. 'Such a naughty boy. So handsome, don't you think?'

'Mmm,' murmured Rose, not wanting to encourage her. Then it suddenly dawned on her that if there was nothing about Angela that made her vulnerable to blackmail, there might be something about her son, and surely a rich and devoted mother would pay anything to suppress a scandal about him.

'But you were asking about my lecture,' Angela went on. 'Mr Steiner is of peasant stock, which makes him more in touch with the earth, the soil, the birds and the bees. But the point of vegetarianism is that it cleanses the body and leaves us free to contact the spirit world. Animals have souls, too. Think of all those poor sheep, pigs and cows slaughtered to feed us.'

'But if we all stopped eating meat,' said Rose, 'all those animals would have to be slaughtered, apart from a very few which would be kept in zoos. Samuel Butler said that if you carry that argument to its logical conclusion, then we would all end up eating nothing but cauliflowers which had been humanely put to death.'

Rose tried not to look at Daisy, who was surreptitiously pouring her tea into a potted plant.

'And,' Rose went on, 'the perception of female beauty would need to change. One is really required to be plump to be considered a beauty.'

'But you see, you are talking of things of the world,' said Angela eagerly. 'We, in my Vegetarian Society, eschew such frivolities.'

'What do the spirits say to you?' asked Daisy. 'I mean, is it like ghosts?'

'No, no.' Angela gave a patronizing titter. 'I shall quote the great Mr Steiner. "Common sense which is not led astray can decide of itself whether the element of truth rules in what anyone says. If someone speaks of spiritual worlds, you must take account of everything: the manner of speaking, the seriousness with which things are treated, the logic which is developed, and so on, and then it will be possible to judge whether what is presented as information about the spiritual world is charlatanism, or whether it has foundation."'

'I don't understand,' said Daisy.

'Oh, I do,' Rose put in quickly. 'This is fascinating. Is your son a vegetarian as well?'

'Alas, no. But he will come round. We females mature very quickly and can grasp metaphysical concepts much better than gentlemen can. May I hope you will join our society?'

'I should like that very much.'

'The subscription fee is two guineas.'

'I will get my father's secretary to send you the money,' said Rose.

'You want Jarvis to do what?' roared the earl at dinner that night.

'It's a very interesting concept, Pa. I think we would all be better off eating vegetables.'

'If you are interested in her son, I would drop that interest now,' said Lady Polly. 'Mrs Barrington-Bruce telephoned me to ask how you were and I told her you were visiting Mrs Stockton. "Keep her away from that place" is what she said. "The son is not to be trusted."'

'But I promised!'

'Then un-promise.'

The earl glared at his daughter. He felt he was almost beginning to dislike her. She was so beautiful and yet all she did was run around behaving in a weird way and putting her reputation at risk. He signalled to the butler. 'Nothing but vegetables for Lady Rose and Miss Levine from now on.'

'Very good, my lord.'

CHAPTER SIX

Mad, bad, and dangerous to know
Lady Caroline Lamb

Three weeks went past without Harry finding a single clue. Rose went to parties and the theatre, wondering all the time what Harry was doing and why he had not tried to contact her.

Lady Polly had not hired a lady's maid for her, saying that Humphrey would help out. Everywhere that Rose and Daisy went, Humphrey went too, watching, always watching.

It was useless to complain. Lady Polly was delighted that her daughter was at last behaving like a débutante, and as Humphrey was quick to claim the credit for this, she praised her lady's maid and urged her on to further effort.

She did not know that Humphrey had a sinister reason for watching her daughter closely.

Humphrey had been attending the consulting rooms of Dr Thomas McWhirter in Harley Street. He was a handsome middle-aged man with thick white hair and a square, tanned face. He had very piercing blue eyes which Humphrey felt could look into her very soul. She had poured out all her resentment against Daisy and the 'strain' of keeping an eye on Rose. She was encouraged to talk about Rose.

At her last consultation, Dr McWhirter had said in that deep, attractive voice of his, 'I think Lady Rose may be insane, cleverly insane. I think she needs treatment.'

'Do you mean Lady Rose should consult you?'

'No, she would be too cunning. I have an asylum, more a refuge, for members of society. It is more like a country house. Lady Polly should be persuaded that it would help her daughter immensely to be confined for, say, a few months. After that, I promise you, she would be a model of society.'

'If I suggest such a thing to her ladyship, I think she would fire me,' said Humphrey.

'But you say your charge gets into serious trouble. Wait for the next episode and seize the chance.'

Rose was not aware she was being courted. A baronet, Sir Richard Devizes, was frequently at her side. As Sir Richard was nearly fifty, the nearly twenty-year-old Rose never for one moment considered his attention to be other than fatherly. And so she allowed him to escort her to his box at the opera and sat with him at soirées and parties.

Daisy tried to caution her but Rose only laughed and said he kept the other men away and he was too old to be romantically interested in her.

It came as a shock to her on the fourth week since Angela Stockton's lecture when her mother and Humphrey burst into her room where she was reading and told her she must put on her best gown because Sir Richard had something important to say to her.

Lady Polly was elated. Sir Richard had asked to pay his addresses to Rose. He was handsome and fabulously wealthy. Certainly he was a bit old, but the guidance of an older man was just what Rose needed. It would also mean that she and the earl could stop worrying about their wayward daughter.

'Why does he want to see me?' asked Rose as Lady Polly and Humphrey fussed over her.

'It's a surprise,' said Lady Polly.

With a sinking feeling in her heart, Rose went downstairs, her silk petticoats rustling beneath a gown of blue taffeta. She missed Daisy, but Daisy had gone to Hatchards to buy her some more books.

Lady Polly pushed her daughter into the drawing-room and left her to face Sir Richard alone.

'Sir Richard,' said Rose nervously, 'why have you called?'

He pulled out a large handkerchief and placed it on the floor and then knelt on it. 'Come here,' he said.

'Why are you kneeling on the floor?'

'Because I am going to propose marriage to you, you lucky, lucky child.'

'Please rise, Sir Richard. I do not wish to get married.'

He struggled to his feet and looked at her in amazement. Then he smiled. 'Ah, you are teasing me. Your sex was always wilful.'

'Sir Richard, I have enjoyed our friendship, that I admit, but I did not think for a moment that your feelings were of a warmer nature.'

He looked at her in amazement. 'Do you mean you are actually refusing me? It would restore your damaged reputation.'

'I do not have a damaged reputation.'

'Anyone who has supported the suffragettes has a damaged reputation.'

The previous year, Rose's photograph, taken at a suffragette rally, had appeared in the *Daily Mail*.

'Sir Richard, I do not wish to be unkind. I find your proposal flattering. But there is a great difference in age.'

'What do you mean? I look like a man in his thirties.'

'It is pointless to stand here arguing,' said Rose. 'I am so very sorry, but I must refuse.' She dropped him a curtsy and hurried out of the room.

Lady Polly and the earl and Humphrey were standing outside the door. Rose rushed past them and up the stairs.

Sir Richard emerged. 'Your daughter is mad,' he pronounced. And Humphrey saw her chance.

'No, no, my dear Lord and Lady Hadshire,' said Dr McWhirter later that day. 'It is not an asylum. It is for people with nervous disorders. Two months under my care and your daughter would be restored to obedience and sanity. The place is called The Grange, just outside Barnet. Like a country house.'

The earl and countess faced him, each thinking that two months without worrying about Rose would be a treat. They could get rid of Daisy Levine, of whom they had never approved.

The earl cleared his throat. 'We could have her back for the beginning of the season, hey?'

'Of course.'

'But she would never go.'

'You do not tell her where she is going. Simply tell her you want her to make a call on an old friend of yours. Shall we say tomorrow morning? I shall be there personally to receive her.'

'I'd feel better if we told Cathcart what was happening,' said the earl.

'We'll phone him when we get home.'

So the earl phoned but Miss Jubbles said that Captain Cathcart was not in his office but she would tell him as soon as he returned.

Harry came out of his office just as Miss Jubbles was putting the phone down.

'Who was that?' he asked.

'Just someone who wanted you to find her lost dog. I told her you were not taking any cases at the moment.'

'Quite right. I'm off to Scotland Yard.'

'No further forward,' said Kerridge gloomily.

'Not traced the owner of the pistol?'

'There are so many arms around after the Boer War and this one was used in the Boer War, as far as we know. It's a German-made Mauser, Model 1896. You know that weapon?'

'Of course. It was called the "Broomhandle". Clumsy thing but deadly. Carries ten 7.63mm rounds in its magazine. It's a more dangerous weapon than the normal six-shot Webley. Hardly a ladies' weapon.'

'I told you I got that statement out of Baker-Willis which gives Lord Alfred an alibi.'

'Where were they all when Freddy was shot?'

'I went back and got statements from them all despite their threats to have me removed from my job. Lord Alfred was dining with – guess who?'

'Tristram Baker-Willis.'

'Right.'

'And Mrs Stockton?'

'Giving a lecture in a side room at the Café Royal.'

'Mrs Jerry?'

'No alibi. Says she can't remember what she was doing. I sometimes wonder if the three of them were in it together. I'd like to see how they act.'

'I think I might find a way to arrange that,' said Harry. 'Lady Glensheil owes me a favour. I could get her to invite all three to a house party.'

'Where? In Scotland?'

'No, in Surrey. She has several residences.'

'Wish you could get me an invitation as well.'

'Not possible. But I could get Lady Rose and Daisy invited. She knows Mrs Stockton.'

'Go ahead with my blessing,' said Kerridge. 'I'm blessed if I can find a single clue.'

* * *

Daisy was feeling uneasy. At dinner that evening, to her surprise, neither the earl nor countess referred to Sir Richard; in fact, they seemed quite affectionate towards their daughter.

But she sensed an underlying apprehension coming from them; and why, earlier, had Humphrey kept shooting triumphant glances in her direction?

'My dear,' said Lady Polly, to her daughter over the floating island pudding, 'I want you to visit an old friend of mine who is poorly. I would like you to go tomorrow morning.'

'Certainly.'

'Humphrey will go with you. Daisy may stay here. I have certain chores I wish her to perform.'

Rose felt so guilty at disappointing her parents that she would have agreed to pretty much anything.

Next morning, Daisy stood at the window and watched Rose and Humphrey being taken away in the earl's carriage. Lady Polly summoned her.

'I want you to pack up my daughter's clothes and things. She will be staying with this friend of mine for a couple of months.'

'But she said nothing of it to me!' exclaimed Daisy.

'Your services are no longer required. We will give you a good settlement. You have two days to pack up and leave.'

Daisy opened her mouth to howl a protest. Something very odd was going on here. Rose's parting words had been: 'I suppose I shall be back sometime in the afternoon. I hope this old lady is not a bore.'

So Daisy said meekly, 'As you wish, my lady.'

'You are a good girl,' said the countess, relieved that there were no protests. 'But you will be more at home with your own kind. You are not one of us and never will be.'

Daisy left and went round to the mews and waited and waited for the earl's carriage to return.

At last, she saw it turning into the mews.

As the coachman, John Silver, descended, Daisy went up to him and asked, 'Where is my lady?'

'Gone into the country.'

'Where?'

'Can't say.' He turned away.

Daisy turned to the two footmen who were getting down from the backstrap. Charles, the head footman, she knew did not approve of her, but Jim, the second footman, had a soft spot for her.

She walked away, determined to get Jim on his own.

She caught him later as he was carrying logs up to the drawing-room. 'Jim,' she hissed, 'where's my lady? What's going on?'

'Told not to breathe a word to you or anyone or I'll get the sack.'

'Please, Jim. The countess has sent me packing and my lady would never let that happen. Please, Jim.'

'All right. But I never told you nothing, mind. Wait till I make up the fire.'

Daisy waited in a fever of impatience until he came out again. 'In here,' said Jim, opening the door of the library. He closed the door behind them and spoke rapidly in a low voice. 'We took her out to a place outside Barnet. It's called The Grange, about two miles out on the North Road. It was a creepy place, with the windows all barred.

'There was a chap with white hair waiting on the step and Humphrey called him Dr McWhirter.

'He and Humphrey led her inside. After ten minutes or so, Humphrey comes out. She says an odd thing, half to herself. She says, "Well, that's settled madam's hash."'

Daisy went to her room and dressed in a warm dress and cloak, a felt hat and boots. She went downstairs and slipped out of the house. She walked through Eaton Square and then through Sloane Square and along the King's Road to Water Street to Harry's address. She hoped she would find him at home. She did not want to go to his office, feeling sure that Miss Jubbles would try to stop her from seeing him.

Becket opened the door to her and Daisy fell into his arms and burst into tears. Harry came out of his front parlour. 'What's the matter?' he asked.

'Don't know, sir,' said Becket.

'Bring her in here and bring brandy.'

Once she had recovered and taken a gulp of brandy, Daisy told them the little she knew.

Harry listened in grim silence. Then he said, 'Let's see what Kerridge knows about this place.'

He phoned Scotland Yard and was put through to the detective superintendent immediately. Harry told him what had happened to Rose, and then asked, 'Do you know anything about this place, The Grange?'

'Do I ever,' sighed Kerridge. 'I was out there on a

sad case. It's an asylum for the rich run by a Dr McWhirter. A certain heiress, Miss Penelope Parry, escaped and got as far as Barnet, crying to the townspeople that she was not mad, that her family had put her away there to get their hands on her money. Police were called. I was called out on it. There was nothing I could do. The family had signed the papers to have her committed and the good Dr McWhirter testified that she was mad. Two days later, she hanged herself in her room. Tragic.'

'I'll see what I can do and let you know,' said Harry.

He put down the receiver and turned to Daisy. 'It's an asylum. What on earth possessed Lady Rose's parents to send her there?'

'They were furious because she turned down a proposal of marriage from Sir Richard Devizes. I think that maid, Humphrey, had something to do with it. Oh, blimey, Humphrey was visiting some doctor in Harley Street for her bleeding nerves.' In her distress, Daisy's Cockney accent was coming back.

'I'll bet,' said Harry, 'that this doctor is a charlatan. I think he hopes to drive Lady Rose mad and have her there for life.'

'Like poor Lady Mordaunt,' wailed Daisy.

Lady Mordaunt's husband had found out that she had been having an affair with the king. So he had taken his pistol, shot all her horses, and had her locked away in a madhouse for life.

'Let me think,' said Harry. 'I know. Daisy, I am going to give you a lesson in lock-picking if it takes all night, and I shall give you some thin files to sew into

107

your clothes. In fact, better sew them into your stays in case they take your outer garments away.

'Tomorrow, I will take you out to The Grange. McWhirter doesn't know me, so I shall use a false name and say you are my mad niece and you must act mad.'

'I'll do anything to save Rose.'

Daisy proved a quick learner in the art of lock-picking and so was able to return to Eaton Square late that evening. She went up to her room and packed a bag. She took off her stays and removed two of the steels and slipped two files in instead. Harry had told her to return and spend the night at Water Street.

Daisy was carrying her bag down the stairs when she found herself confronted by Humphrey.

'And where do you think you're going?' said Humphrey.

'Getting out of here.'

'You are supposed to pack up Lady Rose's things.'

'Pack them yourself, you old trout.'

Rose had never felt so frightened in her life before. She had arrived with Humphrey. Dr McWhirter had met her and said he would take her upstairs to see his 'patient'.

Rose had felt decidedly uneasy. There was the sound of someone sobbing. The stairs were thickly carpeted and the air smelt of cheap cooking and disinfectant. Her mother had said that a Mrs Prothero was an old friend. Still, better get it over with. She would only stay for a few minutes.

Dr McWhirter was joined on the first landing by a burly man in a white coat. 'My assistant, Philips,' he murmured.

He led the way on up and along a corridor at the top of the building and swung open a door. Rose walked into a barely furnished room. There was a narrow bed against one wall. A curtained recess by the window served as a wardrobe. The floor was covered in shiny dark green linoleum.

Rose swung round. Dr McWhirter was standing in the doorway with his powerful-looking assistant.

'Where is Mrs Prothero?' demanded Rose.

'There is no Mrs Prothero. This is an asylum for ladies with fragile nerves. You will be kept here – on instructions from your parents – until we consider you are well again.'

'This is an asylum! I am not mad!'

He wagged a playful finger at her. 'Ah, the mad never know it themselves. But you are in good hands here. If you behave yourself, you will be allowed to join our other guests in the evenings for quiet recreation.'

Rose made a frantic dash for the door, but Dr McWhirter stepped aside and his assistant grabbed hold of Rose, pinned her arms and threw her on the bed. Then they both left, locking the door behind them.

Frightened as she was, Rose could not cry. She was too furious for that. What on earth had possessed her parents to do such a wicked thing? She had heard stories of families who committed their relatives, sometimes to get their hands on a particular relative's money.

But in her case, why?

And then she suddenly thought it was all because she had rejected that proposal of marriage. She was sure her parents had simply meant to teach her a lesson. But she had heard that these places charged high fees. Dr McWhirter probably meant to keep her locked up for life.

The following morning, Harry drove Daisy out to Barnet and parked in front of The Grange.

'Now, Daisy,' he said, 'don't overact.'

'What an awful-looking place,' said Daisy.

'I showed you that place out on the road under the trees. I shall wait there with Becket all today and all night if necessary. If you and Lady Rose are not out by the morning, then I will come in after you somehow. I want to avoid making a scene if possible in case someone calls the police and Lady Rose is embroiled in a scandal again. Good luck, Daisy.'

'You can't call me Daisy anymore,' she said with a show of spirit. 'I am now Miss Levine, companion to Lady Rose.'

'Play your part and it will stay that way.'

Becket helped Daisy down from the car and pressed her hand warmly and she sent him a shy smile.

'How do you know Dr McWhirter is here and not at his consulting rooms?' asked Daisy.

'I telephoned him. Marvellous invention.'

Before he could ring the bell, the door opened and

Dr McWhirter stood there. 'Welcome, Mr Carlisle,' he said. 'And this is the little lady?'

'My niece, Liza.'

Daisy stood shuffling her feet.

'I think it is better if you go away, Mr Carlisle, and leave the young lady with us.'

'But what about the paperwork and fees?'

'I will telephone you. It is better to deal with the patient first and make sure she is happy and rested. Philips, take Miss Liza up to her room. Is that her luggage?' Daisy had packed a few belongings in a suitcase. 'Leave it in the hall.'

Philips took Daisy's hand. She went with him docilely enough, but half-way up the stairs she began to sing at the top of her voice:

Daisy, Daisy, give me your answer, do!
I'm half crazy, all for the love of you.
It won't be a stylish marriage,
I can't afford a carriage . . .

'Shut that row,' snapped Philips as they reached the top of the stairs.

But a voice from a room along the corridor finished the song:

But you'll look sweet, upon the seat
Of a bicycle built for two!

Rose, thought Daisy.

'In here,' said Philips.

'Are you my daddy?' whined Daisy.

He grinned down at her. 'The only daddy you got now.' He thrust her into the room next to the one Rose's voice had come from and closed and locked the door.

Daisy waited until she heard his footsteps retreating along the corridor. She unbuttoned one boot and slid out the thin skeleton keys, re-buttoned her boot and got to work. At first, she'd forgotten all Harry had taught her, but after a few deep breaths she attacked the lock again until there was a satisfying click and she swung the door open.

She peered cautiously along the corridor and then went to Rose's door and got to work. She worked quickly with new confidence and soon had the door unlocked.

Rose, who was sitting on the bed, rushed into her arms and hugged her close.

'How? How did you get here? I heard you singing.'

'Never mind,' whispered Daisy. 'Pooh, it smells bad in here.'

'They wouldn't even let me go to the bathroom. I had to use the chamber-pot under the bed. I haven't even been fed.'

'Shh! Come along quietly.'

They crept together to the top of the stairs and began their descent, both of them glad the stairs were so thickly carpeted. They stood together on the bottom step.

'Right!' said Daisy. 'Straight for the front door as fast as we can.'

But when they got to the door, it was locked and barred. Daisy slid back the well-oiled bolts. She was still clutching her skeleton keys in her hand.

'I'll soon get to work on this,' she whispered.

'Here, you two,' shouted a voice behind them.

They turned slowly and found Philips glaring at them. 'Helga!' he shouted.

A female nurse came out of a side room. She was of the same build as Philips, heavy and menacing.

'Two of our little birds were trying to escape,' said Philips, 'and the doctor's just gone in to London.'

'Lock them down in the basement till he gets back,' said Helga.

Philips grabbed Daisy by the wrist and twisted the keys out of her hand. 'A nasty little spy,' he said.

'I'll have you in court for this,' said Rose and slapped him full across the face.

He hit her on the cheek so hard that she fell to the ground.

'Bastard!' said Daisy, helping Rose up.

'I'll have some fun with you later,' sneered Philips. He took a thick blackjack out of his pocket. 'Now, move.'

'Don't protest,' said Rose, holding her cheek. 'He could crack your head open with that, Daisy.'

A heavy door was opened at the back of the hall. A steep flight of steps led down.

'Get down with you,' growled Philips, 'or I'll shove you down.'

With arms around each other's waists, they went down the stairs as the door slammed above them.

'I can't see a thing,' complained Daisy.

'There's a faint light below.' Rose released Daisy and went ahead, feeling her way down. The staircase curved towards the bottom.

'There's a window, but it's high up and it's barred,' said Rose.

Daisy followed her down and they both stood in the basement and looked around. 'It isn't a cellar. It's a storeroom. Look at all this luggage. It must belong to the other poor creatures in this hellish place.'

'We'll never escape from here,' said Rose.

'I'll try.' To Rose's amazement, in the dim light from the overhead window, she saw Daisy was beginning to take her dress off.

'I've got files in my stays. The captain gave them to me.'

'Oh, thank God. He knows of this.'

'He's outside and if we're not out by morning, he'll come for us.'

'Why doesn't he just bring a gun and blast his way in?' said Rose bitterly.

'Because it's better if we get away quietly. If he shoots his way in, if the police are called, think of the stories in the newspapers. You'd be damned as Mad Rose forever after, no matter what nasty things about Dr McWhirter are uncovered. Here. Help me off with my stays.'

Daisy slid out the files and then put her dress on again. 'Now, how do I get up to that window?'

'We'll need to stack up the luggage and climb up,' said Rose. Heaving and panting, using a cabin trunk as the base, they put suitcase after suitcase on top of it.

Daisy scrambled up and got to work on the bars with one of her files.

'Oh, Rose, this is going to take ages,' she mourned.

'I'll look through the other suitcases,' said Rose, 'and see if I can find something to use as a weapon.'

Daisy worked away diligently while below her, Rose opened case after case. 'Nothing I can use so far,' said Rose. 'How are you getting on?'

'Oh,' wailed Daisy as the file she was using snapped. 'I'll never do this. I've only got one file left.'

'Keep trying,' urged Rose. 'Wait, move away from the window a little. I need light. I think there's a candle here.' Daisy crouched down below the window.

'Yes, and a box of vestas.' Rose struck a match and lit the candle. 'Good,' she said. 'Now I can have a proper search.' For a while there was no sound but the steady rasp of the file. Then Rose, her voice quivering with excitement, said, 'Daisy, you can stop filing. Come and see what I have found.'

Daisy scrambled down the 'ladder' of cases and joined her. 'It's a gun bag with a shotgun and cartridges,' said Rose, her eyes gleaming in the candle-light.

'Do you know how to use it?'

'Yes. I got one of the keepers to show me.'

'But how will that get us through the cellar door?'

'I'll shoot a great big hole in the lock. Hold the candle high while I load this thing.'

Daisy watched, fascinated. 'I never knew ladies had any useful skills at all,' she said.

'Some of us have. There! Now let's cut bits off our petticoats to plug our ears. I don't want to go deaf.

'Now I will fire and reload quickly in case I need to use this on Philips. Believe me, Daisy, I never would dream of killing anyone, but I will kill that man if he gets in my way. It's a double-barrelled shotgun. Let's give that door both barrels.'

Rose hurried up the stairs. Daisy, holding the candle, followed her. 'Back off,' ordered Rose. 'I'm going to fire.'

The resultant blast was tremendous. Not only was the lock shot but there was a jagged gaping hole in the door.

They rushed through. Philips came running down the stairs. Rose quickly reloaded the shotgun and turned to face him.

'Open the front door,' she ordered.

'You'd never use that on me,' said Philips. 'That would be murder.' Because of the ear-plugs, Rose could barely hear what he was saying but she took careful aim and blasted a hole in the step below the one on which Philips was standing. He fell backwards. Rose reloaded. 'Now,' she said, 'open up.'

But he turned and rushed back up the stairs, shouting, 'Helga!'

'That bitch looks as if she might have a gun,' panted Daisy. 'Shoot the front lock.'

Out on the road, Harry exclaimed, 'Becket, I heard shots, coming from the house. We'd better go.'

Becket cranked up the motor and raced along at top speed of thirty miles an hour and into the drive of The Grange.

Rose and Daisy came sprinting down the drive, Rose carrying a shotgun. Behind them came Philips and two other men.

They stopped short at the sight of Harry.

'Get in the car,' shouted Harry.

Rose and Daisy leaped in. Becket turned the car and they drove off.

'I've left me stays,' said Daisy, and burst into tears. Rose hugged her. 'I'll buy you a whole shopful of stays.'

Daisy scrubbed her eyes with her sleeve. 'With roses on the garters?'

'With anything you like.'

At first Rose's parents were outraged by being summoned to Scotland Yard. Surely Scotland Yard should come to them. But when Jarvis told them it concerned their daughter, Lady Polly summoned Humphrey, who was packing up Rose's clothes, and they set out.

When Lady Polly saw her daughter sitting in Kerridge's office, she let out a shriek of dismay. Rose's left eye was nearly closed by the enormous bruise on her cheek.

'What on earth happened?' she cried.

In measured tones, Harry described Rose's ordeal. When he had finished, he said, 'Did you not consider it odd that Lady Rose should be admitted wearing only the clothes she stood up in?'

'They said to send her clothes the following day.'

'And what was she supposed to do in the meantime for clean linen or a nightdress?'

Lady Polly rounded on Humphrey. 'This is all your fault!'

'No, it's not,' said Rose – much to Daisy's disappointment. 'It is you, my unnatural parents. To have me locked up in an asylum because I would not accept a proposal of marriage from a man more than double my age.'

'Here, now. We thought it was a country retreat,' protested the earl. He turned to Kerridge. 'Have you had McWhirter arrested?'

'He is being brought in for questioning and The Grange is being raided. But Lady Rose cannot give evidence in court unless you wish the whole world to know that you considered your daughter mad.'

'This is your sort of job,' said the earl, turning to Harry. 'Cover it up and send me the bill.'

'Were it not for my respect for your daughter, who had to shoot her way out of the place, I would gladly see you exposed in the press. It would be better for you and your daughter if you would accept the fact that she may never get married.'

Rose felt tears welling up in her eyes. She did not know why. 'Don't cry,' said Daisy, pressing her hand.

'I am very hungry,' sobbed Rose. 'We have had nothing to eat.'

'I think you should take your daughter home,' said Kerridge. 'I will call on you this evening when I have found out more.'

That evening, before dinner, Rose met her parents in the drawing-room. Daisy sat quietly in the corner and listened in amazement. She had expected the earl and countess to apologize to their daughter, not realizing that such as the earl and countess did not apologize to anyone, ever.

'We've been thinking, Rose,' said the earl, 'that Cathcart may have the right of it. We have decided to accept that you will probably remain a spinster. Good idea. Save us the expense of another season, what. You always were bookish and interested in odd things like this vegetarian caper. We don't mind so long as you don't go back to supporting the suffragettes or anything scandalous like that.'

'We always try to do what's best for you,' said Lady Polly.

'Such as having me locked up in an asylum?'

'That was Humphrey's fault. I've fired her. Ordered two lady's maids from that new agency. Haven't got time to search around.'

'Humphrey was with you for years,' protested Rose.

'I've given her a good reference and some money to tide her over. More than she deserves.'

'Mama, have you thanked Daisy for saving me?'

'No, but thank you, Levine. Shall we go in to dinner?'

Harry called at his office before going to Eaton Square to hear from Kerridge if McWhirter had been charged.

Miss Jubbles was still there. For the first time, Harry saw the obsessive adoration in her eyes.

He came to a decision. 'Miss Jubbles,' he said, 'you should not be here so late, but I am glad you are. I have something to say to you.'

'Oh, sir!' Miss Jubbles blushed.

I think she expects me to propose to her, thought Harry. This is dreadful.

'Miss Jubbles, I regret to tell you that I have too many overheads and may have to wind up the business. I regret that I do not need your services any longer.'

Miss Jubbles turned as white as she had been red a moment before. 'I will work for nothing!'

'No, I cannot have that. I will pay you three months' wages. That will allow you time to find another position.'

Miss Jubbles looked around in a dazed way at what she had always thought of as 'her room'.

'Becket will drive you home.' Harry opened the window and called down to Becket, who was sitting in the car outside, to come up.

'Becket will call at your home tomorrow with your three months' pay,' said Harry.

Miss Jubbles stood up. She collected her hat and coat from the hat stand and put them on. Then she suddenly fell to her knees and held her hands up as if in prayer.

'Don't send me away. I *love* you!'

'I'll pretend I didn't hear that,' said Harry. 'Ah, Becket, will you please drive Miss Jubbles home?'

Then he turned away and walked into his office and shut the door behind him.

Rose sat silently throughout dinner, her brain in a turmoil. To tell a rebellious spirit like Rose that she was no longer expected to marry made her long to do the opposite. For all her scorn of the season being nothing more than a cattle market, she did nourish romantic dreams of some intelligent man who would sweep her off her feet. Her thoughts strayed to Harry. He never seemed to regard her as a woman. She had a good mind to flirt with him and see if she could break his heart.

CHAPTER SEVEN

He gave way to the queer, savage feeling that sometimes takes by the throat a husband of twenty years' married, when he sees, across the table, the same face of his wedded wife, and knows that, as he has sat facing it, so he must continue to sit until the day of its death or his own.

Rudyard Kipling

Lady Polly had just risen as a signal to Rose and Daisy to join her in the drawing-room and leave her husband to his port when Brum, the butler, announced the arrival of Superintendent Kerridge.

'We'd better all hear what he has to say,' said the earl, getting to his feet.

Both Kerridge and Inspector Judd were waiting in the drawing-room. 'This is a bad business, my lord,' Kerridge was beginning when Harry was announced.

'Ah, Cathcart,' said the earl. 'Come in. Kerridge was just about to start his report.'

Harry stole a glance at Rose. He thought she was looking remarkably beautiful in a dinner gown of oyster satin with white lace panels, despite the bruise on her check.

Kerridge waited until Harry was seated and began again. 'We raided The Grange and found eight people there, all female. They were in a dreadful condition. Most were full of drugs. There was one, a Miss Callum, who had been admitted only the week before. Turns out her parents died and she inherited a considerable estate. Her cousins conspired with McWhirter to have her committed. All ladies have been transferred to Saint George's Hospital for observation. Some were half-starved.

'When we called at Dr McWhirter's consulting rooms, the place was ablaze. There was no chance of recovering any files. The good thing is that if the relatives of the ladies want them to be re-committed somewhere, they will need to apply to me first. A warrant is out for McWhirter's arrest and the ports are being watched.'

He turned his grey gaze on the earl and countess. 'Your daughter is very lucky that she has friends such as Captain Cathcart and Miss Levine or you might never have seen your daughter again.'

'Tish!' protested the earl. 'We were going to call in a few days' time. We would have found out what was up.'

'You would have been told your daughter's condition had deteriorated. You might have been allowed to see her. She might have been heavily drugged, so full of opium, say, that she would look as if her wits had gone. Alarmed, you would press for further treatment, and so it would go on.'

'It's a wicked world,' said Lady Polly, fanning herself so vigorously that little feathers escaped from her ostrich fan and floated in the air.

'Keep a good watch on your daughter,' urged Kerridge. 'McWhirter may still be in the country and he may want vengeance.'

Miss Jubbles felt her heart was broken and her mother was no comfort. Her mother, incensed that her daughter had been the magnet that had drawn Mr Jones to the house so often, told her it was all her own fault.

'How could you even imagine that a man of the captain's class and age would look at you?' she jeered.

So, at the same time as Kerridge was leaving the earl's home, Miss Jubbles put on her coat and hat and went out to get away from the sound of her mother's voice.

There was a warm light spilling out from the rear premises of the bakery. Mr Jones would be busy baking bread and rolls.

The night was chilly and a greasy drizzle was falling. Drawn by the smell of baking bread, Miss Jubbles went round to the back of the bakery and knocked on the door.

Mr Jones opened it. The light shone out from the open door and lit up Miss Jubbles's tear-stained face.

'Whatever's the matter!' he exclaimed. 'Come in. I was just about to take a break.'

Dora averted her eyes. Mr Jones was dressed in a vest and old trousers. Sensing her embarrassment, he took down a white coat from a peg by the door and put it on. 'Come in,' he repeated. 'I've some nice Chelsea buns, and we can have tea.'

Miss Jubbles edged her way cautiously in. There were racks of loaves, rolls and buns sending out a sweet smell.

'George,' said Mr Jones to his assistant, 'make tea. And bring a couple of Chelsea buns. We'll be in the parlour. Come with me, Miss Jubbles.'

Miss Jubbles hesitated, but the thought of going back to her mother made her shudder. So she followed him as he led the way to a little parlour on the first floor.

They sat in awkward silence until George arrived with the tea and buns. Mr Jones went to a sideboard and took out a bottle of brandy. He put a slug of brandy into Miss Jubbles's tea. 'No, don't protest,' he said. 'You look as if you need it. Begin at the beginning.'

He was a good listener. Miss Jubbles poured it all out, stopping occasionally to sip brandy-laced tea and nibble on a warm sugary Chelsea bun.

'It's all that Lady Rose's fault,' she said. 'I'll get my revenge. Tomorrow, I'm going to the *Daily Mail* and tell them how she was masquerading as a common working girl.'

'I wouldn't do that,' said Mr Jones. 'See here, they'll print the story all right . . . Then what happens? Never get on the wrong side of the aristocracy or you'll be finished.'

'But they'll never know it was me.'

'That captain's a detective. He'll find out. He'll remember telling you. What'll he think of you? Now – here, forget the tea, have some more brandy to strengthen you – did he ever, and think carefully, show any signs of being attracted to you in any way?'

'He was very kind.'

'Kind doesn't amount to anything. I was kind to your ma and do you know what happened? She thought I was keen on her and became all twisted and bitter when she found I wasn't.'

Miss Jubbles blinked. 'She said nothing of it to me.'

'Well, she wouldn't. So let's think about this here captain, now. Did he ever press your hand, gaze into your eyes, anything like that?'

A slow blush crept up Miss Jubbles's cheeks. 'Do you mean I imagined the whole thing?'

'Easy done. See here, know why your ma was so furious?'

Miss Jubbles shook her head.

'I told her I was keen on you. Look, see, I imagined you felt warm towards me because that's what I wanted to think. We all get carried away some time or another.'

Miss Jubbles stared at him. Something warmer than the brandy began to course through her veins. She could feel her self-worth gradually being rebuilt in that cosy little parlour, brick by brick.

'Why, Mr Jones! I never dreamt, never imagined . . .'

He took her hand in his. 'You're quite the little heart-breaker . . . Dora.'

* * *

A few days later, Lady Glensheil sent out invitations to a house party at her Surrey residence, Farthings.

Her invitation was received gratefully by Lady Polly. 'It's just what we need,' she said to her husband. 'Get Rose down to the country, fresh air, and away from the fear of that terrible doctor. We shall accept, of course. She has sent me a note with her invitation to say it will be a small party.'

'Still, I wonder who else is going,' said her husband.

'What's in the post?' demanded Mrs Jerry Trumpington across the breakfast table.

Her husband lowered his morning newspaper and looked at her. 'Haven't opened it yet.'

'You're impossible. Give it to me. I don't know why I put up with you.'

He signalled to a footman and handed him the post, which the footman placed next to Mrs Jerry.

Mr Jerry Trumpington surveyed his wife and began to indulge in one of his favourite fantasies. She was a greedy woman. In his mind's eye, she choked on a lump of food. He would sit there calmly, watching her slowly choke to death. That gross body of hers would writhe about and then crash onto the floor like some great diseased tree. He would wait until she gasped her last. A simple funeral. No point in wasting money on the dead. No flowers. What about hymns?

'Here's one!' called his wife down the table. He blinked the dream away and looked at her with something like shock in his eyes because in his mind he was already following the coffin to the graveside.

'What?'

'Lady Glensheil wants us to go to her house party. We must go. She's got a French chef.'

'When is it?'

'Two weeks' time.'

'Bless me. Such short notice. Bit autocratic of her. I've got work in the City anyway.'

Mr Trumpington was director of a tea company. Although tea and beer were not considered trade, Mrs Jerry felt it was rather demeaning of her husband to work at all.

'It'll sound so common, me having to say my husband's working.'

'You spend so much money, I have to keep working. By the way, that gentleman's watch you bought from Asprey's.'

'I told you and told you. That was for nephew Giles.'

'But I saw Giles the other day and he said he had never received such a watch.'

'It must be one of the other nephews. Stop prosing on. It's only a watch.'

'A gold half-hunter is not just an ordinary watch.'

'Oh, shut up about the watch!' she roared.

Her husband bowed his head and went back to arranging her funeral.

Lord Alfred turned Lady Glensheil's invitation over and over in his long fingers. What was an old battleaxe like Lady Glensheil doing sending him an invitation? Still, it would mean getting out of London and away from his creditors. He had lost heavily at the gaming tables and needed to rusticate. Also, if that superintendent from Scotland Yard came calling again, he would find him gone.

'The stage is set,' said Harry a week later. 'The three have accepted.'

'I've looked up Farthings,' said Kerridge. 'There's an inn nearby called The Feathers. I'll book in there the first weekend. Slip out and give me a report. Lady Rose has accepted?'

'Yes, and her parents as well, so I don't suppose she'll be able to be of much help. Lady Rose telephoned me the other day.'

'Aha! You pair getting friendly.'

'I have no interest in a young female who specializes in getting into trouble.'

'If you say so.'

Three days before the house party, Lady Polly contracted a feverish cold. 'I will need to tell Lady Glensheil that we cannot go,' she said.

'Mama, I can go with Daisy. Then there's my new maid, Turner. She will be with us as well. You would not want me to stay in London without your protection while that wicked doctor is still at large.'

'I suppose not. Lady Glensheil is a stickler for etiquette, so don't disgrace yourself. And do try to un-Cockneyfy Daisy. She looked at an artichoke at dinner last night and said, "Am I supposed to eat them bleeding leaves?"'

'If it had not been for Daisy . . .'

'Oh, don't start again. You may go. But behave yourself!'

It was lilac time when Rose, Daisy and Rose's new maid set out for Farthings. More motor cars than ever before were appearing on the streets of London. Rose had originally thought them nasty, smelly, noisy things, but now she looked on them with a jealous eye. She did wish her father would buy one, but he had even refused to buy her a bicycle.

The weather was unusually warm and sunny. The trees and hedgerows were bright green with new leaves forming arches over the road as they drove deeper into the countryside.

Daisy twisted her head round and looked through the window at the back of the carriage. 'There's a car following us. It's been there all the way from London.'

'Probably Captain Cathcart.'

'No, it's not his car.'

'Then it might be one of the other guests.'

'I keep worrying about that doctor.'

'He wouldn't dare come near me. Besides, Captain Cathcart will be there.'

Daisy sometimes felt impatient with Rose. Couldn't she see what a suitable match the captain would make? And then she, Daisy, and Becket could maybe be together.

Harry and Becket, with Becket driving, headed towards Farthings. Two ladies' bicycles were strapped on the back of their car. 'Don't you think, sir, that the earl and countess will consider a bicycle too expensive a present to give an unmarried young lady?'

'I bought one for Daisy as well.'

'Still . . .'

'Lady Rose did tell me on the telephone that she had changed her mind about motor cars but said that her father would not even buy her a bicycle. Stop worrying about it, man. I shall discuss the matter with her, and if she considers the present out of order, she can leave it behind.'

'We'll need to teach them to ride the things,' said Becket.

'I hadn't thought of that.'

Becket suddenly thought of being able to put his arm around Daisy's waist as he helped her learn how to ride, and smiled in the sunshine.

CHAPTER EIGHT

Here we are! here we are!! here we are again!!!
There's Pat and Mac and Tommy and Jack
* and Joe.*
When there's trouble brewing,
When there's something doing,
Are we downhearted?
No! let 'em all come!

Charles Knight

Farthings was a pleasant Elizabethan manor-house. A beautiful old wisteria covered most of the front, its delicate purple blossoms moving gently in the lightest of breezes.

As they went through the usual arrival ritual of being shown to their quarters, Daisy fretted about that car which had been behind them all the way. Whoever was driving it wasn't a guest because it had driven on past the gates. The driver was wearing goggles and a muffler up round his face and he had a cap pulled low down over his forehead.

In her new status as companion, she would no longer eat with the servants and so would have no chance to tell Becket of her fears.

They had been given two bedrooms and a little sitting-room. Rose stood by the window, watching the other arrivals.

'Good heavens, Daisy. There's Tristram Baker-Willis, Freddy's friend. And here comes Mrs Jerry and her husband. You know, I've just thought of something. With Freddy's flat being searched when he was shot, one assumed that the murderer had taken away any incriminating papers. But what if Freddy did not keep any evidence he was using to blackmail in his flat, but had it somewhere else? I must ask the captain. Or, wait a bit, what if the murderer found the evidence, took away his own stuff along with the others and then decided to do a bit of blackmailing himself?'

'There's the dressing gong,' said Daisy.

'The arrivals are going to have to look sharp. Ring the bell for Turner.'

Daisy could never get used to the fact that she was expected to avail herself of Turner's services as well. Not that Turner presented any difficulties. Being lady's maid to an aristocrat was a step up for her. Her last job had been as lady's maid to an elderly widow in Bournemouth. She was in her thirties, polite and correct and self-effacing.

But Daisy loved the luxury of having someone to do her hair and mend and clean her clothes.

When they were ready, Rose in a low-cut white silk gown and Daisy in dark grey silk which Lady Polly considered suitable to her station, they rang the bell for

133

a footman to guide them downstairs, because it was one of those old rambling mansions with many odd staircases.

Lady Glensheil moved forward to meet them, or rather she glided, as if on castors. She was a high-nosed aristocrat with a noble bosom. She was dressed in lilac taffeta and a great rope of black pearls hung round her neck.

'Glad you could come, Lady Rose, and this is . . . ?'

'My companion, Miss Levine.'

'We are a small party. May I present Lord Alfred. Lord Alfred, Lady Rose Summer and Miss Levine.'

'Charmed,' he said in a voice heavy with boredom.

'And Mr Baker-Willis.'

'We've met,' said Rose curtly.

And so the introductions went on. Apart from the suspects, there were two ladies Rose already knew from the house party at Telby Castle, Frederica Sutherland and Maisie Chatterton. She had also met two of the gentlemen before, Sir Gerald Burke and Neddie Freemantle. Harry was the last to arrive.

'That awful bruise has nearly gone, I see,' he remarked.

'I've been wondering what happened to papers or letters or whatever Freddy was using to blackmail people.'

'Maybe the murderer took the stuff away with him.'

Daisy whispered, 'A motor car followed us all the way here.'

Rose laughed. 'Daisy is worried that the horrible doctor is coming after me.'

But Harry did not laugh. 'I'll keep a look-out.'

'Oh dear,' said Rose, looking towards the new arrivals. 'I'd forgotten about them.'

Mrs Angela Stockton and her son came into the room. 'My dear, what *are* you wearing?' demanded Lady Glensheil in ringing tones.

Angela's high-waisted gown looked as if it had been made out of William Morris wallpaper. A huge silver crucifix hung round her neck. Her hennaed hair was topped with what looked like a small green witch's cap.

'I am an aesthete,' said Angela.

'Oh, pooh, greenery-yallery,' said Lady Glensheil. 'At least young Peregrine is properly attired.'

'Tell her we're no longer vegetarians,' hissed Daisy, 'or we'll need to eat nothing but vegetables while we're here.'

'I outrank her,' said Rose, 'so I won't be sitting near her when we dine.'

'But I will,' said Daisy. 'Oh, well, I'll think of something.'

Lord Alfred took Rose in to dinner. Tristram Baker-Willis was seated on her other side.

Rose turned to Tristram first. 'What a terrible business about poor Mr Pomfret.'

'Eh, what? Oh, yes, frightfully sad.'

'Who would do such a thing?'

'Blessed if I know.'

'Probably a burglar,' said Lord Alfred languidly.

'But nothing was taken. I mean, nothing of value.'

'You seem remarkably well informed, Lady Rose.'

'It was in the newspapers. The only thing they did not mention was a servant or servants,' said Rose eagerly. 'Mr Baker Willis, did not Mr Pomfret have a manservant?'

'Yes, he did. Chap called Murphy. But he'd got the night off.'

'And where is he now?'

'How should I know?' demanded Tristram rudely.

'If Lady Rose goes on interrogating us during the meal,' drawled Lord Alfred, 'we won't be able to eat a darned thing.'

Rose noticed Angela Stockton was drinking a great deal of wine. Still, she supposed, wine was vegetarian.

Daisy was tucking into roast beef with pleasure when Angela, defying custom, said right across the table, 'My dear Miss Levine, I thought you were one of us.'

'Lord Hadshire insisted we eat meat. Lady Rose could hardly defy her father.'

'How very sad. Don't you think Lady Rose and my son have a great deal in common?'

'No,' said Daisy bluntly.

Rose watched the three suspects closely after dinner, but there was nothing to show that they had a common problem or, indeed, knew one another very well.

She had pinned her hopes on those three. But what if there had been others? Others who might have paid cash?

Card tables were being set up. 'I think some music would be pleasant as well,' said Lady Glensheil. 'Whom do we have? Why, Miss Levine, I have never heard you sing.'

Rose closed her eyes. She knew Daisy loved to sing.

'Do you want someone to play for you?' asked Lady Glensheil.

'Yes, I would like Becket.'

So Becket was summoned and told to bring his concertina.

Daisy whispered to Becket and then threw back her head and began to sing.

If you saw my little backyard, 'Wot a pretty spot!' you'd
*   cry*
It's a picture on a sunny summer day;
Wiv the turnip tops and cabbages wot people's doesn't buy
I makes it on a Sunday look all gay.
The neighbours finks I grow 'em and you'd fancy you're
*   in Kent,*
Or at Epsom if you gaze into the mews.
It's a wonder as the landlord doesn't want to raise the
*   rent,*
Because we've got such nobby distant views.

Rose suppressed a groan. The card players sat as if frozen. Daisy was getting into her stride, marching up and down and swinging her skirts as she roared into the chorus.

Oh it really is a wery pretty garden
And Chingford to the eastward could be seen;
Wiv a ladder and some glasses
You could see to 'Ackney marshes,
If it wasn't for the houses in between.

Rose and Harry applauded loudly and the others followed suit. 'You do that Cockney bit very well, my dear,' said Lady Glensheil. 'But something more soothing now, I think. Miss Chatterton, perhaps you would oblige?'

Maisie sat down at the piano and began to murder Chopin.

Daisy came and sat next to Rose, her face flushed and her eyes shining. Rose was going to give her a lecture on her behaviour, but then thought that in her music-hall days Daisy had known a freedom denied to society women.

Harry had joined the card players. Rose thought he might at least have joined her. They were, after all, supposed to be investigating this murder. She felt tired and sulky.

'I think I'll retire now,' she said to Daisy.

'Good idea,' agreed Daisy, but only because she had agreed to meet Becket in the gardens later.

Harry covertly watched Rose and Daisy leave the room. What a bore these cards were, he thought. He played another hand and then got up from the table and excused himself.

An hour later, Daisy, with a shawl over her head, waited in the garden at the back of the house. The air was full of the scent of lilac. She jumped nervously as Becket appeared in the darkness beside her.

'I never heard you coming,' she whispered. 'Have you found out anything from the servants?'

'Only that Lord Alfred plays backgammon.'

'So do I!'

'I mean, how shall I put this – he prefers gentlemen to ladies.'

'Ah, now there's something someone could have been blackmailing him about.'

'Exactly. But what sort of proof would they have?'

'There are brothels, you know, for that sort of thing.'

'You've led a rough life.'

Daisy shrugged. 'Comes in handy sometimes.'

'But I still can't see how it would work. Someone goes to Lord Alfred and says, "I saw you go in the door of such-and-such a place." He'd deny it. Can't ask the people who run the place, if it's a high-class one. They keep their trade by shutting up about their clients.'

'Photographs. What about photographs? Someone with one of those Kodak cameras.'

'Could be. If that's the case, I wonder if they were destroyed.'

Daisy sighed. 'I'm beginning to think the murderer did destroy them and that's the end of it. Then the three have alibis. But how do they know what time he was actually killed? Rose told me after dinner that Freddy had given his manservant the night off and yet it was the manservant who found the body.'

'The manservant would sleep there, so he'd come back later – anyway, that's what it said in the newspapers – find Freddy dead and call the police. The manservant left at six in the evening and returned at eleven, so they've been collecting alibis for that time.'

'Where is the manservant? Do we know?'

'I asked the captain. He says the manservant made a statement and then disappeared.'

'Wait a bit, flats like his would have a porter on duty.'

'Porter didn't see anyone apart from the residents. The door to Mr Pomfret's flat wasn't locked. He must have let his murderer in.'

'People must have heard the shot.'

'St James's is a noisy place. The residents above and below were abroad. A Mr George Bruce at the top of the building heard something, which, in retrospect, he believes might have been a shot, but he says at the time he thought it was one of those nasty new-fangled motor cars.

'Mr Kerridge says that the murderer must have shot Freddy as he opened the door and searched frantically through his papers and then ran out.'

'But the porter must have seen someone running out.'

'He says he didn't, but it turns out he often nips round to the pub in St James's Lane. The landlord seems to be a friend of the porter and both are sticking to their stories that the porter wasn't in the pub that evening. Frightened of losing his job.'

'I'd best be getting back,' said Daisy.

Becket was just plucking up courage to kiss her on the cheek when they heard a stifled sneeze in the shrubbery behind them.

'Who's there?' demanded Becket sharply.

He ran towards the shrubbery and parted branches but could see no one.

'Could have been a cat,' said Daisy uneasily.

'Cats don't sneeze like that.' Becket looked uneasily about. 'Let's go inside.'

The country house party developed into a sedate and often boring affair: croquet and cards and long heavy meals.

Harry covertly watched the three suspects. The only thing suspicious about their behaviour could be that they avoided one another. And yet what did they have in common? Lord Alfred could not be expected to enjoy the company of a gross glutton like Mrs Jerry any more than Mrs Stockton would. Nor would he approve of Mrs Stockton with her faddishness and ridiculous clothes.

Her son, Peregrine, was always trying to engage Rose in conversation but she seemed to be successful at snubbing him.

Rose had at first toyed with the idea of flirting with Peregrine to see if she could find out anything about his mother but found the young man too repulsive.

Harry had only the meeting with Kerridge to look forward to.

He had held back from presenting the bicycles to Rose and Daisy, feeling that, after all, the presents were a bit too expensive for a gentleman to present to two unmarried young ladies.

But Rose was being singularly pleasant to him – because she wanted to break his heart although he did not know that. So on the morning of the fourth day of the visit, he said a trifle awkwardly, 'Lady Rose, I may be doing the wrong thing but I did bring you and Daisy a present.'

'What is it?' asked Rose.

'I bought you a bicycle each.'

'Oh, how simply marvellous. Daisy, the captain has bought us bicycles. May we start to learn to ride them right away?'

'You will need to change,' said Harry, looking at Rose's white muslin gown with its flounces and frills.

'Come, Daisy,' said Rose, 'I cannot wait to begin.'

So Becket's dream of holding Daisy's waist while he taught her to ride came true. Both girls were wearing divided skirts, white blouses and straw boaters.

There was a wood on the estate with a bridle path running through it. To the disappointment of both men, the girls proved to be quick learners.

'Daisy and I will go for a run on our own,' said Rose. Only after the pair had gone flying off did Harry regret not having brought bicycles for himself and Becket.

Lady Glensheil came up to them as they were walking back to the house. 'I saw you gentlemen wheeling bicycles. Where are the young ladies?'

'Gone off cycling. They learned very quickly.'

'Oh, this cycling craze,' sighed Lady Glensheil. 'I keep a few for guests.'

'Where?' demanded Harry eagerly.

Lady Glensheil turned to her ever-present maid and footman. She said to the footman, 'Paul, fetch a couple of gentleman's bikes.'

* * *

Rose felt dizzy with happiness as she and Daisy flew down the bridle path. It was such a delicious sense of freedom. At last they stopped. 'I think we should go back,' said Daisy, anxious to see Becket again. 'We didn't even thank the captain properly.'

'Oh, very well.' They turned their bikes around when a man stepped out from the shelter of the trees and held a pistol on them.

'Dr McWhirter,' gasped Rose.

His eyes glowed in the green gloom of the forest with a mad light.

'It was all your fault,' he said. 'You ruined me. Me. I was once the most courted doctor in Mayfair. My business is ruined. I am ruined. But I'll take you with me, you nasty, scheming little bitch.'

Daisy felt she should stand in front of Rose, but that would mean he would shoot both of them. She was terrified and her bladder gave.

He smiled and cocked the pistol.

Harry, speeding along the bridle path with Becket behind him, saw Rose and Daisy, white and petrified, and the figure in front of them. Kerridge had shown him a photograph of McWhirter, and looking at that thick white hair, Harry was sure it was the doctor. With one hand he fished out his own pistol from his pocket. A brief memory of riding a horse in the veldt during the Boer War and leaning forward over the pommel to take aim came back to him.

Praying he hadn't lost his skill as a marksman, he fired directly at the doctor's back.

McWhirter dropped to the ground.

Daisy burst into tears and Becket dismounted and ran to her. Rose stood where she was, very still, staring straight ahead.

Harry dismounted. He knelt down beside McWhirter's body and turned it over.

'Dead,' he pronounced.

He got to his feet. 'Lady Rose,' he said. 'Go back to the house. Do not tell anyone of this.'

Rose said through white lips, 'Why? The police will have to be informed.'

'Well, that's the problem. Why did he attack you of all people?'

'He blamed me for everything. So what are we to do?'

Harry turned his head. 'Becket, go back to the house and find two spades.'

'But this is criminal!' protested Rose as Becket left Daisy, mounted and pedalled off.

'I am trying to avert a scandal. If this became known, your parents would summon you home. One of their servants who had not been in their employ very long might decide to earn some money by talking to the newspapers about your visit to the asylum. It's better this way. Take Daisy and go back to the house.'

'No, I want to see it through to the end,' said Rose.

'But I've wet meself,' wailed Daisy.

A hysterical giggle escaped from Rose's lips. 'Then you go back, Daisy.'

'Not without you.'

They waited uneasily for Becket. 'I hope one of the guests doesn't decide to go for a ride,' said Harry.

At last they saw Becket speeding down the path towards them with two spades balanced on the handlebars.

'Right,' said Harry, taking the spades from Becket. 'Let's drag this body into the woods.'

Daisy and Rose, clutching each other, followed them.

Rose suddenly released Daisy and turned away and vomited.

'That's it,' said Harry. 'Back to the house with both of you. Daisy . . .'

'Miss Levine to you,' said Daisy shakily.

'Miss Levine, take her back and tell anyone who asks that you both have a touch of the sun.'

Daisy and Rose shakily made their way back to their bicycles. They mounted and began to pedal slowly at first and then furiously towards the house.

They handed their bicycles to a footman and went up to the sanctuary of their rooms.

Daisy stripped off and hid her underwear at the bottom of a drawer. She did not want Turner to know she had soiled herself.

After she had bathed and dressed in fresh clothes, she went into Rose's room. Rose was lying on the bed, her eyes half closed.

'I am not very brave,' she said weakly.

'I'm feeling better,' said Daisy in bracing tones. 'That's one fright dealt with.'

'This won't do,' said Harry. 'We can't leave the body here.'

'Why not?' asked Becket.

'No matter how deeply we put it, some animal might start digging and a keeper might find it. Kerridge would immediately connect me with the shooting. All he has to do is check the gun licences for people in Britain with a Webley and my name would come up.'

'How would he know it was a Webley?'

'From the bullet.'

'We could dig the bullet out of him. And why didn't they trace the owner of the gun that shot Pomfret?'

'It was one of the hundreds of unlicensed old Boer War weapons in Britain. Whoever murdered Freddy simply left it lying on the floor beside his body. Whoever killed Freddy knew that weapon could never be traced.'

'So what'll we do?'

'Cover him up with leaves and we'll come back after dark with the car, take it miles from here, and sink it somewhere in the upper reaches of the Thames. Daisy said something about a car following them. We'd better look for McWhirter's car, if it was him, and get rid of it as well.'

Rose and Daisy picked nervously at breakfast the next day. There was no sign of Harry. Both wanted to talk to him about McWhirter – to talk away some of the nightmare.

'You are looking very pale, Lady Rose,' said Maisie Chatterton, who had just helped herself to a large selection from the buffet. She sat down next to Rose.

Rose noticed that Maisie no longer lisped as she had done a year ago. 'This is not a very exciting house party,' mourned Maisie. 'The gentlemen are either boring or quite too simply dreadful. Mr Stockton is a rotter, but at least he shows some interest in the ladies, which is more than can be said for the rest of them. Sir Gerald is as sarcastic as ever. Neddie Freemantle brays as ever. Mr Baker-Willis glooms about the place. Your captain is –'

'He is not my captain,' said Rose.

'Indeed! You seem to be the only lady he talks to. I thought our hostess might have arranged something, but she spends her day reading newspapers and magazines and shows no interest in anyone. I asked her what we were doing today and she said, "Whatever you want." What sort of answer is that from a hostess?'

Rose felt she must escape into the fresh air. 'Excuse me,' she said. 'I am just going outside, Daisy. There is no need for you to join me.'

Outside, Rose stood and breathed deeply. The day was glorious. Not a cloud in the sky and the trees were still bright spring-green. She heard a step behind her and swung round nervously.

Tristram Baker-Willis came up to her. 'Jolly day, what. Care for a walk?'

'Why not?' said Rose.

They walked round to the back of the house, where formal gardens ran down to an ornamental lake.

'Oh, look, swans,' said Tristram.

Two swans were standing on the grass beside the lake. 'How ugly they look out of the water,' said Rose.

'I say, I never noticed that before. You're a jolly observant girl.'

What is he after? wondered Rose.

'Sad business about Freddy,' said Tristram, snapping off the head of a rose. He looked at it in amazement, as if wondering how it had got on his hand, and then shrugged and tossed it to the ground.

'Yes, very sad,' agreed Rose.

'What's Cathcart doing here? He still poking his nose into business that should be dealt with by Scotland Yard?'

'I do not know. I think he is simply here as a guest. Lady Glensheil is very fond of him.'

'Something deuced creepy about a fellow sinking to such a trade. I'm surprised that Lady Glensheil should encourage him. All of society should shun him.'

Where is Harry? fretted Rose.

Then she suddenly stopped short. Today was the day when Kerridge would be at The Feathers. Harry had probably gone to see him alone.

'Must go,' said Rose, and picking up her skirts, she ran back towards the house.

Daisy was not in the breakfast room. Rose ran up the stairs and found Daisy in their private sitting-room, looking out of the window.

'We'd better change and get those bicycles,' panted Rose. 'I had forgotten. Kerridge is at that inn called The Feathers today. Ah, Turner, there you are. We are going cycling. We will need our divided skirts, blouses and hats.'

Soon they were speeding down the drive after a wobbly start. 'Where is The Feathers?' shouted Daisy.

'I saw it when we came through that little village. It's only about a mile from the gates.'

When they reached the inn, the landlord informed them that Mr Kerridge was in the pub garden at the back.

And there they found Kerridge eating a large breakfast, with Harry and Becket beside him.

'You might have told me you were going to meet Mr Kerridge,' accused Rose.

'I thought you were asleep,' said Harry wearily. He had not been to sleep, having driven all night to get rid of the body and the car and then having come straight to the inn.

'So is there any news?' demanded Rose.

'Sir Andrew Fairchild, the king's equerry, volunteered the information that Mr Pomfret had approached him with a view to buying a title.'

'And what did Sir Andrew say to that?' asked Rose.

'Of course he pretended to be shocked and said titles were never bought, which was silly of him, as everyone knows they are these days. So that confirms Mr Pomfret's father's story that Pomfret was desperate for a title. We studied the bank accounts further. He did not have much money, or rather, he did not keep much money. Very extravagant spender.'

Harry put his hand over his mouth to hide a cavernous yawn.

'Didn't you get any sleep?' asked Kerridge.

'Not much. Went for a drive.'

'Near a river?'

'I beg your pardon.'

'Your car has mud on the sides and yet the weather is still fine and dry.'

'Oh, we came through a water splash. Where was it, Becket?'

'I cannot recall, sir. One village at night is very like another village. Have you learned anything, Lady Rose?'

'Not really. On the face of it, it is an exceptionally boring house party. Everyone just glooms around. Lady Glensheil has obviously considered that having supplied a theatre for your suspects, she does not need to do anything more about it. Oh, Mr Baker-Willis invited me for a walk this morning. He was anxious to find out why Captain Cathcart was included in the guest list. I said it was because you were a friend of Lady Glensheil. He seemed highly nervous and ill at ease.'

Kerridge looked disappointed. 'I was hoping something more dramatic would have happened by now.' Rose and Harry exchanged glances.

'What's that?' demanded Kerridge. 'Has something happened?'

'Nothing at all,' said Harry quickly.

'There's no sign of McWhirter,' said Kerridge, fixing Rose with a hard stare.

Rose felt herself beginning to blush.

'You haven't seen him?'

'If we had seen him, we would of course have contacted the nearest police station,' said Harry smoothly.

Kerridge leaned back in his chair. He wagged a finger at Harry. 'You've been up to something. You haven't shaved. You've got bags under your eyes. And you've got mud on your car.'

Harry thought quickly. 'I went for a drive all night because I could not sleep. I was in the Boer War, you know. It's the reports in the papers of Kitchener's concentration camps in South Africa packed with starving women and children. For us British to behave like that is sickening. It is tantamount to treason to criticize our glorious victory, but I would see those donkeys of leaders, Buller, Kitchener and Lord Roberts, in the dock for having caused so much death and misery. Thanks to the new photograph reporting showing pictures of the misery of the Boer women and children, we are the shame of the world.'

There was a long silence. A wasp settled on the remains of Kerridge's breakfast. At last, the superintendent said gruffly, 'I'll still be here tomorrow in case you can find out more. If one of them took whatever evidence of their misdeeds when they shot Mr Pomfret, they might have that evidence with them.'

'I'll see what I can find,' said Harry.

Outside the inn, before she mounted her bicycle, Rose said, 'We could search their rooms. There is a game of croquet scheduled for this afternoon. Everyone usually plays. I could get into Mrs Jerry's and Mrs Stockton's rooms and you could try Lord Alfred.'

'Leave it,' said Harry curtly. 'You've already been in too much danger.'

But Rose was determined. Despite Daisy's pleas to be careful, Rose waited until everyone was assembled on the lawn for the game of croquet and then excused herself, saying the sun had given her a headache.

She went straight to Mrs Jerry's rooms. They were easy to find because, in the usual way, cards were on each door with the names of the occupants. It was an apartment like the one she shared with Daisy: two bedrooms off a sitting-room.

There was a desk by the window in the sitting-room. She went to it and began to search through the small amount of papers. They were mostly unpaid bills and letters.

And then she heard someone in the corridor outside. She hid behind a curtain and waited, her heart beating hard. The door opened and she heard Mrs Jerry's voice, obviously speaking to her husband.

'It's a stupid game, the sun's hot and I'm tired.'

'Then go and lie down' came her husband's voice.

'What are you going to do?'

'What do you care?'

'Don't be so grumpy, popsy-wopsy. Come here.'

Perspiration began to form on Rose's brow.

'No, I won't,' said Mr Jerry. 'It's too buggering hot.'

'Language!'

'Coming from someone who swears like a fishwife, that's rich!'

There was the sound of a slap, and then Mr Jerry said evenly, 'Do that again and I'll kill you, you fat, disgusting toad.'

'You! Don't make me laugh. I'm off to bed.'

Rose heard the bedroom door slam. She waited and

waited. She could hear Mr Jerry moving about and then the creak of a chair as he sat down.

After fifteen minutes of agony, there came a rumbling snore from the bedroom.

Then to her horror, she heard Mr Jerry say, 'You can come out now. She's asleep.'

Blushing furiously, Rose emerged from behind the curtain.

'I came in to borrow a book,' she said in a low voice.

'I saw your feet under the curtain. Let's go for a walk,' he said amiably.

Rose followed him out of the room and down the stairs. 'We'll go out onto the terrace at the back,' said Mr Jerry. 'You know, I didn't want to come. I told my wife I had business in the City to attend to. But she did screech so. She doesn't like me, so why she wanted me along is beyond me. Ah, here we are. Nice and cool. Let's sit down instead while you explain why you were spying. You were thick as thieves last year with Captain Cathcart during that business at Telby Castle, so I suppose the pair of you are up to something.'

Rose decided it would be better to tell the truth. 'Your wife paid Mr Pomfret the sum of ten thousand pounds. I think Pomfret might have been blackmailing her.'

'I challenged my wife over that. She said it was a loan.'

'Mrs Stockton and Lord Alfred also paid Pomfret ten thousand pounds each,' said Rose.

'Blackmail! Oh, my dear, if only that were true,' he exclaimed.

'Why?'

'Don't you see, if it were indeed something so awful that she paid out that great sum of money and if I got my hands on it, I could divorce her. Captain Cathcart is investigating the murder, is he not?'

'Yes.'

'Then I shall offer to pay him anything he wants to find me proof.'

'Can you think what it might be?'

'A man, perhaps. But what man? I mean, look at my wife. I will go back and search for you. And I will talk to Captain Cathcart later.'

'I am so sorry I hid in your room.'

'Don't worry about it. You have given me hope.'

CHAPTER NINE

*Even if we take matrimony at its lowest, even if
we regard it as no more than a sort of friendship
recognised by the police ...*

*Times are changed with him who marries; there
are no more by-path meadows, where you may
innocently linger but the road lies long and
straight and dusty to the grave.*

Robert Louis Stevenson

Dinner on the previous nights had been long, dull
affairs. The guests mostly concentrated on the
delicious food and largely ignored each other.

Lady Glensheil did not notice, mainly because she
liked the sound of her own voice and filled in the long
gaps with monologues about the state of the nation, the
weather, and the difficulties of getting good outdoor
staff. She would probably have complained about the
difficulty of getting good indoor staff had not so many
of them been waiting on the guests.

That evening, however, began badly over the soup

and proceeded to get worse. Mr Jerry Trumpington had already been drinking quite a lot. His shoulders were usually hunched like a man expecting another blow, but for once he was sitting up straight. There were two hectic red circles on his cheeks.

'What a jolly bunch we are!' he cried.

'Oh, do be quiet, *dear*,' admonished his wife.

'No, I won't be quiet. For once in my bullied married life I won't be quiet, you fat old frump.'

'Mr Jerry, perhaps you would like to lie down?' said Lady Glensheil in glacial tones.

'No, I'm fine and dandy. The prison door has opened a crack. Do you know why we're all here, hey?' He pointed with his dripping soup spoon, first at his wife, then at Angela Stockton and Lord Alfred. 'See those three? Each one of them paid the late and unlamented Freddy Pomfret ten thousand pounds. Blackmail, I think. So, dear wife, if the murderer and blackmailer is amongst us, I beg of him to supply me with whatever he has on my dear wife and I will pay him a fortune.'

Harry glared at Rose, who dropped her eyes to her plate.

'You're drunk,' said Lord Alfred coldly. 'If you can't hold your wine, go to bed and stop making ridiculous accusations. The police have already questioned us. It is sheer coincidence that we all decided to help Freddy out. He demanded the same amount from each of us.'

'Oh, Lady Rose!' squeaked Maisie Chatterton. 'Don't tell me there's going to be another death. Death does seem to follow you around.'

'I'll talk to you later,' Mrs Jerry snarled. Mr Jerry merely grinned.

'Listen to me, all of you,' said Lady Glensheil. 'We are all going to church in the morning, and I mean all. Now, let's talk about something else. The situation in the Balkans is fraught . . .'

Her voice rose and fell inexorably through eight courses before she finally rose as a signal to the ladies to follow her to the drawing-room. But she turned in the doorway. 'I think this evening we will break with tradition and the gentlemen will come as well.'

To everyone's relief, Mr Jerry said he was going to bed. In the drawing-room, tables were set up for cards while Frederica Sutherland entertained them by singing Scottish songs and accompanying herself on the piano.

Harry drew Rose aside. 'Why did you tell Jerry about the blackmail?'

So Rose told him about being caught hiding behind the curtain.

'You shouldn't have said anything,' said Harry crossly. 'Now they really will be on their guard.'

'Oh, pooh!' said Rose defiantly. 'They must already have thought it odd that all three of them have been invited. Did you find anything in Lord Alfred's rooms?'

'Nothing incriminating.'

'Did you bury the body very deep?'

'No, we didn't bury it. We took it off away to the Thames with his car and sank the both of them.'

'So Daisy was right. He must have been following us. Where was the car?'

157

'Outside the gates.'

'But someone will find the body in the river.'

'Don't worry. The water was pitch-black and we wedged him behind the steering wheel of his car.'

Philip Hargraves, a blacksmith and motor mechanic, was walking along the upper reaches of the Thames outside the village of Maidenton with his teenaged son, Bertie, just as the sun was coming up. He planned to get in some early fishing before starting work.

It was a truly beautiful morning and the dawn chorus sounded from the trees along the grassy bank.

'Look at that, Dad,' said Bertie, stopping short. 'Tyre tracks going straight into the river.'

Philip joined his son and together they looked down into the waters of the Thames. The water may have been pitch-black at night, but in the brightening rays of the sun it was still and clear along the stretch outside the village. There was a strong current in midstream, but by the bank the water was as clear as glass.

And so, looking down, they were able to see a figure in a car sitting on the bottom.

'Better call the police,' said Bert.

'No, wait a bit,' said his father. 'Let's get that car out first. I'll go back and get the tractor and winch it out. You keep a look-out.'

'But, Dad!'

'Do as you're told or I'll take my belt to you!'

The motor car and body were slowly winched up out of the Thames.

Philip's face was red with excitement. 'Let's get this

back afore anyone sees us,' he said. 'Hop in the tractor.'

'But, Dad, the body.'

'I'll tell you about that.'

Philip drove carefully back to his smithy, looking carefully left to right to make sure no one was watching. It was still very early and his smithy was on the outskirts of the village.

Outside the smithy, he unhitched the motor car and pushed it inside. 'Now, you,' he said ferociously to his son, 'not a word of this or I'll beat the living daylights out of you. Run along. You say one word and I'll get to hear of it. Poor gentleman probably was drunk and drove straight into the river.'

The boy scampered off. Philip shut the double doors of the smithy and locked and bolted them. Then he stood and stared at the car in delight. It was a Spyker six-cylinder engine, four-wheel drive. Other cars only had rear-wheel brakes. He had seen a photograph of it in the *London Illustrated News* showing it parked outside the Crystal Palace. The Spyker factory was in Trompenburg, Amsterdam. The family name was Spijker, but the firm's name was Spyker, largely because the motor cars were exported to English-speaking countries.

He was itching to get to work on it, but first he had to get rid of that body. He unlocked the doors of the smithy and peered out. No one around. He went to the stables and hitched up the pony to the trap. Then, with his powerful arms, he lugged the dead and wet body of McWhirter and threw it in the back and covered it with sacking. The river had washed the blood away and swollen the corpse, so he did not, in his excitement, notice the bullet-hole in the back. He relocked the smithy and left a note on the door to say he would be back later.

He set off, driving steadily through the sunny, leafy lanes, his heart singing with gladness. There was a generous God in heaven who had sent him a Spyker.

He made a leisurely journey, stopping often to rest and water the pony. At last he saw a thickly wooded area beside the main road with a sandy track running into it and drove along the track to where the trees and underbrush were dense.

He heaved the body out of the cart and carried it over to a large tree and propped it up against the trunk. The dead man was wearing an expensive watch but he decided not to take it. The beautiful car was enough. He would tell the villagers that a gentleman had left it with him for repairs and had never come back.

The following morning Mr Jerry awoke with a groan. His head ached and he could hear the pounding of the breakfast gong. Normally guests rose when they felt like it, but this was Sunday and Lady Glensheil was determined that all should breakfast early and go to church.

Little flashes of his behaviour at the dinner table came into his mind and he groaned and pulled the quilt up over his ears. No doubt his wife would be in shortly to scream at him. Until then, he would enjoy as much peace and quiet as he could.

His valet entered quietly and said, 'Wake up, sir. Her ladyship wishes your presence in the dining-room.'

'Tell her I'm sick,' he moaned. 'Tell her I'm dead.'

'What about Mrs Trumpington? Her lady's maid says her door is locked and she cannot rouse her.'

'She's probably dead as well. Go away!'

He tried to get to sleep again, but, aware of another presence in the room, feebly opened his eyes.

His wife's maid, Bartlett, was looming over him. She was a powerful woman and he was almost as frightened of her as he was of his wife.

'What are you doing in my room?' he demanded, struggling up against the pillows and then groaning and clutching his head.

'I cannot get into madam's room. The door is locked and she expressly told me to rouse her in time for the church service.'

'I'm sure they've got spare keys to all the rooms in the servants' quarters. Now, LEAVE ME ALONE!'

The church was small and old, smelling strongly of essence of villager, because the sun striking in through the stained-glass window was heating up the crowded congregation.

The vicar was frightened of Lady Glensheil, and in an effort to please her had written a very long sermon indeed. And as the sermon had to do with helping the poor and Lady Glensheil firmly believed the poor had brought their poverty on themselves by drink and gambling, she glared at the vicar from under the shadow of an enormous straw hat laden with waxed fruit. Lady Glensheil was often attacked by petty meanness and she had instructed her maid to take the waxed fruit out of the bowl on the dining-room sideboard and attach it to her black straw hat. Although the maid had stitched diligently, attaching the fruit by putting a net over each piece, each item was heavy. A banana detached itself and fell on to Lady Glensheil's lap, to be followed by an apple.

'I wish something would happen to make that tiresome man finish his sermon,' she said.

The door of the church suddenly burst open and Bartlett rushed in, shrieking, 'She's dead! My mistress is dead. He killed her!'

That shut the vicar up. The congregation sprang to its feet.

'Good thing Kerridge is here,' said Harry, who was next to Rose. 'I'll go and fetch him.'

Mr Jerry had risen and locked his own bedroom door. He climbed back into bed and sank down under the covers. Peace at last.

Then he heard a frantic rattling at the doorknob and Bartlett crying, 'Murderer. I'm getting the police.'

'Ghastly rotten, rotten creature,' he muttered. He closed his eyes and blessed sleep came at last.

He awoke half an hour later. Someone was shaking him. He blinked and looked up. Detective Superintendent Kerridge, having obtained the spare key from the servants' hall and flanked by Captain Cathcart, was staring down at him.

'What the blazes . . .' he began.

'Please get dressed, sir,' said Kerridge. 'Your wife is dead.'

'She is? I mean, how? Choke on some food? Always was a greedy woman.'

'No, sir. Mrs Trumpington has been strangled.'

'Good Gad! Here, hand me that dressing-gown. Where's my man? I must get shaved.'

'Mr Trumpington, that can wait. We have questions we must ask you immediately.'

Now thoroughly frightened and with his mind racing, Mr Jerry got out of bed and put on his dressing-gown and slippers. What had happened last night? What had he done? He could remember her shouting at him. Then all was blank.

While he sat down in his private sitting-room, Harry went back into the bedroom. Mrs Jerry was lying there, her eyes protruding and her tongue sticking out. He averted his eyes and turned his attention to the bedside table. There was a champagne bottle there. He peered down into it. It was empty. He looked down into the wastepaper basket.

There were several scrunched-up pieces of paper and a champagne cork. He smoothed out the pieces of paper but they were merely notes reminding Mrs Jerry about jobs to give to her maid, like mending a tear in a gown and checking the inventory of the lace box.

Two local policemen entered the room. 'What are you doing here, sir?'

'I have the superintendent's permission.' Harry was about to turn away, but then he frowned and stooped and picked up the champagne cork. He looked at the dead body again. She hadn't struggled. Although fat, she had been a powerful woman. Surely she would have thrashed around as she fought for her life.

He produced a magnifying glass from his pocket and studied the cork. There was a little hole in the top. He went quickly into the sitting-room and interrupted Kerridge's interrogation of Mr Jerry.

'Come over here to the window,' said Harry, 'and look at this. Here, take my magnifying glass.'

Kerridge peered at it. 'What's up with it?'

'That tiny little hole. She didn't struggle. She may have been drugged. Someone could have taken a hypodermic syringe and injected some sort of drug into the bottle.'

'But why go to such lengths?'

'To stop her making a noise.'

'We'll need to wait for the results of a full post-mortem to find out. I wonder how the door got locked on the inside.'

'Easy,' said Harry. 'Bartlett said she got the spare key from the servants' hall. Therefore our murderer must have done the same thing. Maybe he meant to return later and make sure he hadn't left any clues.'

'Were you all in church?'

'All except Mr Trumpington here. Look at him. I really think he was out for the count all night. Oh, I've just remembered something. He told the dinner table last night that he knew about the blackmail and that he would pay a fortune for the evidence against his wife.'

'How did he know?'

'Lady Rose told him.'

'I should arrest him now.'

'If it were simply a matter of her being strangled in a drunken rage, perhaps I might believe he did it. But I firmly believe she was drugged first.'

Kerridge turned to the crumpled figure of Mr Jerry. 'Go to your room, sir. We will wish to question you further.'

'Come into the bedroom,' said Harry. 'As far as I remember, there wasn't a glass.'

'Maybe the maid took it away.'

But when Bartlett was summoned, she said she had not touched anything.

'No glass,' mused Harry. 'Of course she was greedy enough to drink from the bottle. It must have been someone she knew and wasn't frightened of.'

'Like the husband?'

'I'm sure it's someone else.' Harry went to the window and opened it. Then he bent and sniffed.

'Smell this. I think after she had been drugged, our murderer poured the contents of the champagne that was left out into the garden and some of it splashed on the sill.'

'There are reinforcements arriving,' said Kerridge. 'I'll have all their rooms searched.'

'Tell your men to look for a hypodermic.'

'You should have put gloves on before you touched that window.'

Harry sighed. 'If you think this lot are going to let you take their fingerprints without a direct order from the prime minister, then you are very much mistaken.'

* * *

'I wish I were a man,' said Rose fiercely to Daisy.

'Why?'

'Captain Cathcart is up there with the police, being informed of everything. We just have to wait until he deigns to tell us something.'

'I wonder why she was killed?' said Daisy. 'If she was killed and didn't choke to death shoving food in her mouth.'

'I'm sure it's murder. I wonder if she knew who the murderer of Freddy Pomfret was. Just suppose he collected the evidence against her when he shot Freddy and decided to do a bit of blackmailing himself. He goes to her and she tells him she's had enough and is going to tell the police. What else could he do but murder her?'

'I wish we could get out of here,' mourned Daisy. 'I'm frightened to death, I can tell you. Telby Castle seems exciting now, looking back on that murder last year, but at the time I was scared and unhappy, and I'm scared and unhappy now.'

Rose gave her a quick hug and Daisy looked at her in surprise. Rose was normally not given to demonstrations of affection.

'I sent a footman off with a telegram to my parents,' said Rose, 'which means that they will shortly arrive to remove me from here as soon as possible and the field will be left to Captain Cathcart.'

'The press will be here soon as well,' said Daisy.

'Perhaps not. I think that Scotland Yard will want to keep this quiet as long as possible.'

'They can't,' said Daisy. 'All the village was there when that maid burst into the church crying murder.'

'Oh, I've just thought of something.' Rose bit her lip in vexation. 'They'll be searching all around the country-side just in case it was someone from outside. What if they come across McWhirter's body in the Thames? Then it will all come out, me being in the asylum.'

Far away, a poacher was making his way through a thick wood. He had no fear of meeting a keeper. The keepers hardly ever patrolled these woods and his pockets were empty of game.

He came across a dead man propped up against a tree. He stood stock-still. Crows and foxes had already begun their destructive work. And then he noticed how the sunlight shafting through the trees glinted on the gold watch on the man's wrist. He bent down and removed it and tucked it into his rags. Then he searched the pockets and found a wallet in the inside pocket. The money inside was wet. He scratched his head. It hadn't been raining for days. Still, the notes could be dried out.

He felt the cloth of the man's motoring coat. Good material. It would fetch a bit at the pawn.

He rolled the body until he got the coat off. A good coat and trousers and silk waistcoat were revealed.

He looked quickly around, but the wood was completely silent. He busily got to work. The river had washed all the blood away and he was disappointed to find a hole in the back of the coat. But, undeterred, he stripped off and dressed himself in the corpse's clothes and then, heaving and panting, dressed the corpse in his own rags.

Then, gagging slightly at the smell from the already decomposing body, he dragged it farther deep into the wood and covered it with leaves.

'It's all right,' Harry reassured a still worried Rose later that day. 'Becket and I took the body really far away and the water was deep and black.'

Rose said, 'The water would be black at night. What if it's clear during the day?'

'Oh, it'll be fine,' said Harry, although he suddenly felt uneasy. 'Have you been interviewed yet?'

She shook her head. They were standing together outside the house on the front lawn. A tendril of hair floated loose from Rose's elaborate hair-style. He felt a tug at his heart but quickly reminded himself how infuriating Rose could be with her unfeminine independence.

Harry had told her as much as he knew.

'If only it could have been someone from outside,' said Rose. 'Have you seen Daisy?'

'I think she's talking to Becket.'

'She is not much use as a companion at times. She should be on duty.'

'Not the little radical you try to be,' said Harry. 'When the chips are down, you are as class-ridden as anyone in society.'

'That is not true, you hateful man.'

Harry looked ruefully after her as she walked away.

A footman came out of the house and said Lady Glensheil wished to speak to him.

Her ladyship was in the morning-room. Mr Jerry

was sitting on a sofa beside her and she was holding his hand.

'Ah, here you are,' she trumpeted. 'Not much of a detective, are you?'

'There was no way I could anticipate this murder,' protested Harry. 'Mrs Trumpington was a suspect . . . I'm sorry, Jerry.'

'It's all right,' he said gloomily. 'If she hadn't been murdered and left me as the prime suspect I would be celebrating, and there's no use pretending otherwise. She wasn't always like that, you know. When I married her, she was a pretty little slip of a thing and I thought myself the luckiest man in England. Don't get married, Harry. They all turn out the same.'

'I beg your pardon,' said Lady Glensheil frostily. 'I am married.'

'But Glensheil's never around, is he?' said Mr Jerry, made tactless in his distress.

'Never mind that. Captain Harry, you must do something about this dreadful business before we are all murdered in our beds.'

'I will do my best. Kerridge is a brilliant policeman.'

'Nonsense, the man's as thick as two planks.'

'His manner and appearance are deceptive.'

The butler entered. 'The police wish to interview you now, my lady. They are in the estate office, as you wished.'

'Very well.' She rose majestically to her feet and adjusted her hat. After having given her lady's maid a row over the waxed-fruit disaster, Lady Glensheil had changed all her clothes, feeling that a new outfit was called for in such distressing circumstances. Lady Glensheil never went hatless during the day. She was wearing a broad-brimmed felt hat decorated with a stuffed seagull with small ruby eyes.

She turned in the doorway and glared at Harry. 'Do something,' she snapped. 'You're a detective, so detect!'

After she had gone, Harry turned to Mr Jerry. 'Have you the slightest idea what your wife could have been up to that would make her the target of blackmail?'

'Can't think.'

'Could she have been having an affair?'

'I don't know. I was in India last year for a few months. Maybe then. But who would want her?'

'It's the evidence that Freddy had. Did the murderer find it? Or did Freddy have it hidden somewhere?'

'Blessed if I know. Wait a bit. We put valuables in safe-deposit boxes at the bank.'

'Surely the police thought of that when they were going through his bank accounts.'

'Might have come under a different department at the bank.'

'I'll use the phone. Blast! There isn't one, and its Sunday anyway. I'd better see Kerridge.'

Harry nearly collided with Lady Glensheil as she emerged from the estate office.

'Have you done anything yet?' she demanded.

'Give me time,' said Harry patiently.

He went into the office. Kerridge was seated behind a desk, with Inspector Judd, stationed in a corner, holding a large notebook on his knee.

'I've just had an idea,' said Harry. 'Look, Pomfret may have put any blackmail evidence in a safe-deposit box at the bank.'

'Lady Rose Summer,' announced the policeman who was on duty outside the door.

'Come in and sit down, Lady Rose,' said Kerridge. He thought she looked a picture. She was wearing a white lace blouse with a high boned collar and a dark skirt of some silky material which rustled when she walked.

'No,' he said to Harry. 'We did check that. Mr Pomfret did not have a safe-deposit box.'

'Now that Mrs Trumpington is dead,' said Rose, 'perhaps it might be an idea to check if Mrs Stockton or Lord Alfred have been paying out any large sums of money recently. You see, if whoever murdered Freddy took blackmail material, he might have decided to go into business himself.'

'Yes,' said Kerridge, 'but that assumes that the murderer is someone other than the two of them. But we'll check anyway. Now, Lady Rose, before I start to question you on this case, you haven't seen anyone suspicious lurking around?'

'What other case?'

'Dr McWhirter.'

'Oh.' Rose exchanged a glance with Harry and said quickly, 'No, not a sight of the man.'

She suddenly remembered McWhirter as he had stood pointing the gun at her and then the sight of his dead body. She turned pale, gave a choked little sound, said, 'Excuse me,' and ran from the room.

Kerridge leaned back in his chair and studied Harry's face. 'I've always known Lady Rose to be exceptionally brave, but when I mention McWhirter she nearly faints.'

'I think she's suffering from delayed shock,' said Harry. 'The fact that her parents put her in an asylum was a terrible fright. It distressed her no end.'

'If you say so. Never take the law into your own hands, Captain Cathcart, or I will treat you like a common criminal.'

'Of course,' said Harry blandly. 'Are we all confined to the house?'

'Yes, until I finish my investigations. Why?'

'I wanted to go up to my office to see if there are any messages for me.'

'Got someone there on a Sunday to take them?'

'No,' said Harry, defeated. All at once he regretted having told Miss Jubbles about Rose and hoped against hope she would keep her mouth shut. But he was determined to find a way to get back to where he had put the body and the car in the Thames to make absolutely sure no one could see anything from the river bank.

Old Mrs Jubbles lived in a perpetual rage. Her daughter, Dora Jubbles, of whom she had held such high hopes, had announced her engagement to the baker, Mr Jones.

She had proceeded to make her daughter's life as much of a living hell as she could manage and Miss Jubbles had retaliated by leaving home to live in sin with the baker until the wedding in several weeks' time.

Miss Jubbles had moved out that very Sunday morning. Mrs Jubbles sat alone, all her hatred turned against Lady Rose Summer. It was that society bitch who had turned the captain against her Dora. If it had not been for her, Dora would never have stooped so low as to marry a mere baker. In her choler, Mrs Jubbles forgot that she had entertained hopes of marrying Mr Jones herself.

And then her anger left her as she saw a plan of action. She would take a hansom down to the *Daily Mail* offices in Fleet Street and tell them the whole story about how Lady Rose had been working as a common typist.

She summoned Elsie, the maid of all work, to help her dress in her best. Despite the warmth of the day, she put on her squirrel fur coat and her new lavender dogskin gloves.

At the newspaper's front desk, she only told them that she had a society scandal to tell the editor. She was told to take a seat.

Mrs Jubbles waited. It was very warm. She opened her coat and saw to her dismay that there was a milk stain on the front of her best gown and hurriedly closed it again.

At last she was ushered up. The news-room seemed to be hectic with excitement. Mrs Jubbles did not know that one of the villagers had wired the paper about the murder at Farthings.

She was escorted in to see the editor. 'I believe you have a story for us.'

173

'How much?' she demanded.

'It depends what you story is ... Mrs Jubbles,' added the editor, consulting a slip of paper with her name on it which had been sent up from the front desk. 'May we offer you some tea and may I take your coat?'

'I would like tea, yes, but I'll keep my coat on.'

The sun was streaming in through the windows of the office. Sweat began to trickle down Mrs Jubbles's face.

The editor waited until tea was brought in and then said, 'Now, what's all this about?'

'It's about that ... that ...' Mrs Jubbles clutched her throat.

'Madam, I fear the heat is making you ill. Do let me take your coat.'

'No, no. It's that awful girl. My daughter, oh, my daughter.'

And unconsciously echoing Shylock, Mrs Jubbles suffered a massive heart attack and fell from her chair and then lay as dead as the animals which had gone into the making of her best fur coat.

'Well, that's that,' sighed Kerridge when the last interview was over. 'Unless the servants tell Garret, who's interviewing them, something interesting, we're no further forward. All the guests and Lady Glensheil claim they were fast asleep. No one ordered a bottle of champagne. No syringe found in the rooms anywhere. Maybe Cathcart or Lady Rose can come up with something.'

'If you will forgive me for saying so, sir,' ventured Judd, 'it surprises me that you should share the investigation with amateurs.'

'I'll tell you why. It's because amateurs are lucky. I sometimes think they could get away with murder.'

With Becket driving, Harry guided him to the place where they had shoved the car with the body of Mr McWhirter into the river. The grey light of dawn was spreading across the country-side despite the banks of clouds building up over their heads and the dawn chorus was starting up.

Philip had left no tell-tale tracks. Rather, he had returned and driven the tractor up and down the river bank to obscure any motor-car tracks. A stiff wind was blowing, whipping up waves across the river.

They stood on the edge of the bank and looked down. But the water was so turbulent now that they could not see a thing.

'There you are,' said Harry with relief. 'See how black the water is?'

'It's going to rain,' said Becket, looking up at the black clouds. 'I wonder what it's like here on a calm, sunny day.'

'Never mind. I assure you there's nothing to see. We've gotten away with it.'

CHAPTER TEN

*It is a mistake to suppose that eating and
drinking stimulate conversation at the moment.
We know that not until the champagne has gone
at least twice round the tables are our tongues
loosened; and this unlocking process is not a
pretty one.*

Macmillan's Magazine, 1906

Dinner that evening started off silently. Even
Lady's Glensheil's tongue was silent. Her black
gown was decorated with so much jet that it glittered
like the skin of some primeval reptile.

The men were wearing black armbands and the
ladies had looked out their darkest clothes. For the
young women of the party, Rose, Daisy, Maisie and
Frederica, it had been hard to find anything suitable to
wear, débutantes usually being attired for evening in
white or pastels.

Daisy was the most decorous in her grey silk. Rose
was wearing lilac silk, but with a dark purple shawl

about her shoulders. Maisie's maid had stitched black edging on a lime-green gown and Frederica had embellished her white gown with a tartan sash as if for a highland ball, thinking that a show of native Scottishness showed enough respect for the dead.

Everyone began to drink more than usual. The acidulous Sir Gerald Burke was the first to give tongue. People said he had become nastier after that business of extricating himself from the clutches of a middle-aged American lady. Gerald had wrongly assumed the lady to be an heiress and, on finding she was not, had proceeded to retreat, followed by her loud and public recriminations.

'I don't know why we are all being kept here,' he complained. 'It's all your fault, Jerry.'

'What, me? I didn't murder her, old chap.'

'You wanted rid of her. Why not just own up and let us all go home?'

Harry decided to see if he could shake them. 'I don't think it could possibly be Jerry,' he said. 'I mean, he was four sheets to the wind last night. His hand wouldn't have been steady enough to inject the drug into the champagne bottle.'

All eyes turned on him. Angela Stockton, resplendent in acres of black velvet and a black cap, looked like an actress playing Hamlet's aunt. 'You're being ridiculous,' she said. 'Isn't he, Peregrine?'

'Talking tosh,' mumbled her son. 'We've got to get out of here or we'll all go mad.'

He had reason to be worried. The night before, when Mrs Jerry was choking out her last breath, he had been busy seducing a buxom kitchen maid. The girl had cried afterwards and said she had sinned and he was terrified she would tell Lady Glensheil before he had a chance to put some miles between himself and the old battleaxe.

'No,' said Harry calmly. 'Mrs Jerry did not struggle before she died. There was an empty champagne bottle beside the bed. The cork was in the wastepaper basket and it had a fine hole pierced in it.'

There was an alarmed silence. The general consensus of opinion of everyone except Rose and Daisy was that the much-goaded Jerry had lost his rag in a drunken rage and throttled his wife and they didn't blame him one bit. 'Would have done it myself if I'd been married to a bullying horror like her,' Neddie Freemantle had said earlier.

'I do not like everyone shouting across the table,' said Lady Glensheil. 'Kindly confine your conversations to the people on your right or on your left.'

No one paid any attention to her.

'You know what I think?' asked Tristram Baker-Willis ponderously.

'No, we don't,' snapped Sir Gerald. 'None of us thinks you *can* think.'

Tristram ignored him. 'I think it's all balderdash and tosh about poor old Freddy being a blackmailer.' He fastened his gaze upon Rose. 'You never liked him. That's why you started this rumour about blackmail.'

'That's not true!' said Rose. 'How do you explain three people paying him ten thousand pounds each and now one of them is murdered?'

'We all know Jerry strangled his wife,' said Tristram.

'I say, steady the buffs.' Neddie Freemantle.

'Enough!' shouted Lady Glensheil. 'We will now talk about something else!'

That evening she was wearing a small jewelled cap embellished with ostrich feathers and those very feathers appeared to bristle with outrage.

They all felt silent, poking at their food like bad children and covertly studying one another.

There was a general feeling of relief when she rose to lead the ladies to the drawing-room. They were crossing the hall when a small kitchen maid curtsied and addressed Angela Stockton. 'Mum, I got to speak to you.'

'What are you doing abovestairs, Miss Whatever-your-name is?' barked Lady Glensheil.

'I got to be done right by,' whined the maid. She pointed at Angela. 'Her son done took my cherry.'

'What has this to do with fruit?' demanded her ladyship.

'I'll deal with it,' said Angela hurriedly.

She stepped forward and took the girl by the arm and hustled her into an ante-room.

'What's this about, girl?'

'Your son bedded with me last night.'

'You must have led him on!'

'Not me, mum. I feel I ought to go to the perlice. After all, a fellow who ruins a poor girl like me must be up to worst.'

Angela slumped down in a chair.

'What's your name?' she demanded.

'Alice Turvey, mum.'

'How much?'

'I don't rightly understand, mum.'

'You want money, don't you? How much?'

Alice put her apron up to her face to dab her dry eyes while figures ran through her head. 'Two hunner' guineas,' she finally gasped out.

'You shall have it,' said Angela wearily.

'When?'

'Now. Come to my rooms. But you must leave this house.' Angela always carried a great deal of money with her.

Alice bobbed a curtsy and followed her. Ten minutes later she ran down the stairs to the servants' quarters and signalled to the pot-boy, who followed her out the kitchen door.

'Did you get it?' he asked.

'Two hunner' guineas,' said Alice triumphantly.

'Told you she'd pay up. When d'you get the money?'

'I got it.'

'Good. I'll steal what I can and we'll get out of here tonight. It's off to 'merica for us.'

'But the police might stop us.'

'Easy. You've been fired, that's what you'll say, and I'm helping you with your bag.'

Kerridge started the interviews all over again the following day but his researches were interrupted as various guests came in to complain they had been robbed. Lord Alfred said his gold cigarette case was missing, Lady Glensheil could not find a silver buttonhook, Maisie screeched that her pearl necklace had gone, Tristram Baker-Willis said he had been robbed of twenty pounds which he had left in his dressing-table drawer and the others complained of expensive trifles that had been taken from their rooms. Only Rose's and Harry's rooms had been left untouched.

It was quickly established that both the kitchen maid and the pot-boy were gone. A shame-faced policeman on guard outside the gates to keep the press at bay said he had questioned the couple when they left the estate but they both said they had been dismissed and the young girl had cried most touchingly.

Irritated, Kerridge started the hunt for the missing couple.

And Lady Rose Summer received a proposal of marriage.

She was walking in the gardens to take the air. The morning's rain had cleared but the clouds were still thick overhead and a stiff wind was blowing. Daisy had just grumbled that it was too nasty to be outside and Rose had sent her away.

She heard someone calling her name and turned round. Tristram Baker-Willis came up to her. 'Lady Rose, I have been trying to have a word in private with you.'

'Go ahead,' said Rose. 'Is it something to do with these murders?'

'No. And such a pretty lady as yourself should not be troubling your head with such awful things. I blame

Captain Cathcart. He's always whispering to you. Is there something between you?'

'Nothing at all,' snapped Rose.

'You see – this is jolly difficult – I've fallen most awfully terribly in love with you and I want you to be my wife.'

Rose stared at him in amazement. 'Why?'

'I just told you,' he said in tones of exasperation. 'You're making this awfully difficult for a chap.'

'Mr Baker-Willis,' said Rose, 'I fear the fright of these murders is making you behave in a strange way. My parents have told me to return to London as soon as possible. But although you should have asked my parents' permission first before proposing to me, I can give you my answer. I barely know you and, no, I do not wish to marry you or anyone else here.'

He kicked moodily at the sodden earth of a flower-bed. 'I may be your last chance.'

'What are you talking about?'

'You know you're called the Ice Queen and chaps say you talk like an encyclopedia. I don't mind all that, but most chaps would.'

'I am getting cold, Mr Baker-Willis. I find your proposal unflattering. If you will excuse me . . .'

She hurried away from him round the house and nearly collided with Harry.

'Whoa!' he exclaimed. 'What's all the rush?'

'Mr Baker-Willis has just proposed marriage to me.'

'Has he, by Jove? Why on earth would he do that?'

'Get out of my way, you stupid man,' shouted Rose. She pushed past him and stalked into the house.

* * *

'And Captain Harry *dared* to wonder why anyone would propose to *me*,' raged Rose to Daisy a few minutes later.

'It does seem odd.'

'Not you, too!'

'I mean,' said Daisy, 'it's not odd that a gentleman should propose to you. Only if the gentleman happens to be Mr Baker-Willis. He hasn't been making sheep's eyes at you. Why the sudden interest?'

'I have a very large dowry,' said Rose in a small voice, her anger evaporating.

'That's probably it. A lot of those fellows are always looking for an heiress. And a title draws them like a magnet.'

'Oh dear,' said Rose. 'I called Captain Harry stupid. I thought he was saying I was too ugly to attract a proposal from anyone, including himself.'

Harry and Becket were summoned to the estate office to face an angry Kerridge.

'Sit down, both of you,' said Kerridge heavily. 'I had a man on the gate last night. You pair drove out past him. He said he didn't stop you or question you going or returning because the idiot assumed you had my permission. I distinctly told him to let no one past. But, oh, no, he touched his helmet as you go off and then he lets two thieving servants away as well.'

Anxious to divert Kerridge's attention from themselves, Harry said, 'There was evidently some fuss last night when the ladies left the drawing-room. Becket here says it was the talk of the servants' hall. Peregrine

Stockton had seduced a kitchen maid. Angela Stockton led her off into a side-room. I would assume she paid her off. She and the pot-boy obviously decided to help themselves to a few trinkets as well while we were all the in the drawing-room.'

But Kerridge was not to be distracted. 'So where did you go last night?'

'I motored to London to pick up my letters and came straight back. I did not think I was a suspect.'

'Everyone's a suspect, even you,' said Kerridge nastily. 'Don't ever leave here again until this investigation is finished. We have wired all worried parents and relatives to stay away. If I cannot find anything out today, I will need to let them all go.'

To Rose's distress, Tristram seemed to have come to the conclusion that his proposal had been too abrupt and so he set about courting her. His method of doing this was to praise her fulsomely and throw her languishing glances.

She could only be glad that her parents had decided to stay in London, having been informed by the police that she would only be required to stay at Farthings for, perhaps, another day. Rose felt sure that if they had arrived on the scene and if Tristram had asked their permission to pay his addresses, and *if* she proved to have turned down another eligible gentleman, they would, she knew, be furious.

What the newspapers were saying about it all, no one knew, Lady Glensheil having stopped the delivery.

No one wanted to chat or socialize or play croquet any more. Suspicion hung like a black cloud over Farthings.

Guests and staff were painstakingly interviewed over and over again. More detectives arrived, discreetly dressed, to search the whole house.

'They won't find anything,' said Daisy to Rose. 'I bet our murderer, if he took any blackmailing evidence, has got it neatly hidden somewhere in London.'

'Mrs Stockton and Lord Alfred really must be sticking hard to their stories about paying Freddy ten thousand pounds out of the goodness of their hearts,' said Rose. 'I only saw them talking together once and eavesdropped. It seems that Lady Glensheil is so determined to put an end to all this that when Kerridge got permission to search their homes in London, they could do nothing to stop it, because she has more influence in high places than either of them. But although they seemed furious at the intrusion, neither of them seemed particularly worried that the police would find anything.'

'When I was growing up in the East End,' mused Daisy, 'there never was any privacy. And one day after the show at Butler's, this stage-door Johnny gave me a box of chocolates. I knew if my brothers and sisters saw that, I'd never get any. So I hid it up the chimney. Wouldn't you know it? Next day was a cold snap and Ma lit a fire and the whole box tumbled down into the flames.'

Rose stared at her. 'Daisy, I wonder if the police searched up the chimneys?'

'Let's go and put it to Kerridge.'

'No, wait a bit.' Rose was desperate to prove to Harry that she was better at detecting than anyone else. 'The police would announce they were searching the rooms again. One of the servants would see them searching up the chimneys and the news would go around like wildfire. I know, at dinner tonight I'll suddenly say I feel faint. You help me out of the room.'

'I'll help you make up to look pale,' said Daisy eagerly.

'Not white lead. I do not know why women will still use that cosmetic. So many of them die of lead poisoning.'

Harry fretted over the soup at dinner. He kept stealing glances at Rose. She was so very white and there were blue shadows under her eyes.

Then he heard Rose mutter an excuse and rise from the table. She left the room, supported by Daisy. Harry, being neither relative nor husband, had to remain where he was and resist the impulse to run out of the dining-room to find out what was wrong with her.

'Now,' whispered Rose as they made their way up the stairs. 'Mrs Stockton's room first.'

There was no electricity laid on at Farthings, nor gaslight, and so they had taken one of the bed candles from the hall table to enable them to read the names on the cards on each door.

'Here we are,' said Rose at last. 'Let's hope her maid is in the servants' hall.'

Rose had a stab of worry that the door might prove

to be locked, particularly after all the petty thefts, but to her relief it opened. Oil lamps were burning in the little sitting-room, so she blew out the candle.

'I'll look,' said Daisy. 'If anything's hidden, it'll be on the little ledge above the hearth.'

'These are Tudor chimneys,' Rose pointed out. 'They probably go straight up. Don't take off your evening gloves, Daisy. If there's anything there, we don't want to leave fingerprints.'

Daisy crouched down on the hearth and reached up into the chimney. She felt around. 'Nothing,' she declared, sitting back on her heels. She tried the bedroom chimney, but there was nothing there either.

'Let's hurry and try Lord Alfred's chimney.'

Another search along the old twisting corridors until they found Lord Alfred's room.

'I'll be as quick as I can,' said Daisy. 'I don't want that manservant of his returning and finding us. He frightens me.'

Again, she knelt down to search up a chimney.

'Nothing here either.' She then searched the bed-room chimney. Nothing but soot.

'It was a mad idea anyway,' said Rose. 'I know, let's try Mr Jerry's room, or rather, his wife's bedroom. If the killer was in a hurry, he might have hidden it there.'

'Hurry, hurry,' urged Daisy. 'Don't want to get caught.'

Rose felt a frisson of fear as she opened the late Mrs Jerry's bedroom door. Of course the body had been removed, but somehow the air still smelt of the patchouli that Mrs Jerry liked to spray on herself.

Daisy went quickly to the chimney. Again, her searching fingers couldn't find anything. 'Let's get out of here,' she urged.

Back in their sitting-room, Daisy stripped off her sooty gloves. 'Turner will wonder what I've been up to.'

'Just tell her you dropped a brooch in the grate and you were looking for it.'

'She'll wonder why I didn't just unbutton them at the wrist and peel them back like we do in the dining-room.'

'Forget Turner. Let me think. Of course. The killer would hardly stand in front of her and inject whatever drug it was into the champagne bottle. He, or she, would take the bottle to their room. People don't normally carry syringes around with them. So whoever it was must have come prepared. But why? Did Mrs Jerry threaten the murderer in London?'

She went to the window and looked out. 'If he – let's assume it's a he – threw the syringe out of the window it would land in one of the flower-beds below. But I'm not thinking clearly. Whoever it was would not need to get rid of the syringe right away. He would only do it later after Captain Cathcart made his announcement in the dining-room about the champagne bottle. Unless it was actually in his pocket – no, it wouldn't be there. A servant might find it. So he goes up to his room as soon as he can. He must have had it hidden somewhere very clever because the police had already searched the rooms.'

'He might not have thrown it out of the window,' said Daisy. 'If he leaned out, he could hide it in that thick wisteria.'

'Well, we can't start climbing up ladders to look for it without occasioning comment,' said Rose. 'If we got up at dawn, the sun strikes full on the front of the house and we might see the rays shining on the glass of the syringe. I'll tell Turner that we are leaving for a walk very early and we can dress ourselves.'

There was a knock at the door. Daisy opened it. Harry stood there with Becket.

'I came to see how you were feeling, Lady Rose,' he said.

'Oh, I'm fine now,' said Rose airily. 'It was the heat in the dining-room.'

Daisy was disappointed. Rose was obviously not going to tell them about the search for the syringe, so they would not be joining the early-morning hunt.

'As long as you are well,' said Harry. His eyes moved to the sooty pair of gloves Daisy had left on a side table. 'Someone been cleaning out the fireplace with evening gloves on?' he asked.

'Silly of me,' said Daisy, not meeting his eye. 'I dropped a brooch in the grate and scrabbled about for it.'

Harry's eyes moved to the grate. Because of the warm weather, the fireplace had been cleaned and was now decorated with leaves and pine cones.

'I found it,' Daisy went on hurriedly.

'They're up to something,' said Harry as he and Becket walked down the stairs. 'Why would Daisy's gloves be covered in soot?'

'Miss Levine may have been searching up the

189

chimneys looking for the blackmail material. I had forgotten, people sometimes hide things up chimneys when the fires are not being lit.'

'I'll suggest that to Kerridge tomorrow. But why did she not tell me? Lady Rose will put herself in danger if she decides to detect on her own.'

Rose had a restless night. She was frightened of oversleeping. But as soon as they pale grey light of dawn filtered in through the curtains, she got up and roused Daisy.

They dressed and made their way down the stairs. 'I hope there is sun this morning,' whispered Rose. 'It was overcast yesterday.'

They stood together on the lawn and waited. The sky was clear, with only a few wisps of cloud, which turned pink in the rays of the rising sun.

Their eyes swept along the thick wisteria which covered the front of the house.

'There!' whispered Rose, clutching Daisy's arm in excitement. 'There's something sparkling amongst the leaves half-way up. Let's tell Kerridge.'

'He's at The Feathers and the policeman at the gate won't let us past,' said Daisy. 'The press are probably still lurking about. He usually comes here at eight in the morning. Not long to wait.'

Daisy suddenly grasped Rose's arm. 'I think someone was watching us, I saw a curtain twitch.'

'Let's get back inside and wait for Kerridge,' said Rose, looking uneasily up at the windows. 'I can't see anything.'

* * *

Harry went in to see Kerridge just after eight o'clock and found Rose and Daisy already there. 'These young ladies,' said Kerridge, 'had the idea that our murderer may have dropped the syringe into the wisteria. You were right about the drugging. The preliminary autopsy confirms that she was drugged with a powerful sleeping-potion. I've sent my men to get ladders. Come with me, Lady Rose, and point out exactly where you think you saw something shining in the leaves.'

Harry was furious. Rose had lied to him. He followed them out, angrily reminding himself that he had never really liked her anyway.

As Harry stood apart from her, his hands behind his back, and his brows down, Rose felt ashamed of herself. She went up to him. 'I would have told you the truth but I thought you would think my idea silly.'

'No, you didn't,' he said curtly. 'You wanted to prove that you were better at detecting than I.'

He walked a little way away from her.

'I thought *you* might have told me,' said Becket to Daisy.

Daisy shrugged. 'If she won't, I can't.'

Rose pointed to where she had seen something shining. Kerridge told the policemen to put the ladder up against the house at that point and begin the search.

Rose kept glancing at Harry's set face. She knew in that instant that anything he found out about the case he would keep to himself in future.

The policeman on the ladder gave a shout. 'I see it!'

'Lift it with your hankie,' shouted Kerridge. 'Don't want your prints on it. Is it a syringe?'

'Yes.'

Kerridge turned to Rose. 'Good work, my lady,' he said. 'We should have you on the force.'

Then he turned to Harry. 'Let's go inside. I want to discuss this.'

He waited until the policeman had climbed down the ladder and then he and Harry walked off together, followed by Becket and Inspector Judd.

'Just look at them!' raged Rose. 'I find their evidence, but because I'm a woman they never think that I should be part of their rotten discussion. When I return to London I shall contact the suffragettes and support them once more.'

'I'll get my men to search this place from top to bottom,' Kerridge said to Harry in the estate office. 'Then I'll need to let them all go. Lady Glensheil has tried to help, but I am now being leaned on heavily from above. Oh, yes, they want me to solve the case but without upsetting the nobs. And this old place has so many nooks and crannies.'

Come the revolution, thought Kerridge, this would make a good orphanage and this lot would be out there working in the kitchens and gardens. He had a vision of Lady Glensheil scrubbing the pots in the kitchen with a piece of sackcloth as an apron tied round her waist.

'Mr Kerridge,' said Harry sharply.

'Eh, what? Oh, yes, I don't suppose there will be prints on that syringe.'

A policeman entered. 'Whose window was it under, lad?' asked Kerridge.

'It was under the window on the first-floor landing.'

Kerridge sighed. 'So any one of them could have thrown it out as they went up or down the stairs. Blast! Are you sure, Captain Cathcart, that neither Mrs Stockton nor Lord Alfred have been particularly friendly?'

'Not that I have seen. None of them are particularly what I would call friendly, except perhaps Tristram Baker-Willis, who has proposed to Lady Rose. Probably after her title and money.'

Kerridge looked amused. 'Why do you jump to that conclusion? Lady Rose is very beautiful.'

'Lady Rose is irritating and unfeminine.'

'I would have said you both had a lot in common.'

'Tommy-rot!'

The fact that they were all told they could leave on the following morning had lightened spirits considerably and an air of relief pervaded the dining-table.

Only Rose felt unhappy because Harry would not look at her and Tristram kept breathing compliments in her ear.

She was glad when Lady Glensheil finally rose to lead the ladies to the drawing-room. Maisie and Frederica spoke of the coming season. Maisie said that if she did not 'take' at this, her second season, she would be sent to India. Frederica said roundly that she had half a mind not to get married at all. There weren't any decent chaps on offer. Lady Glensheil said loftily it was the duty of every young miss to marry. There was no other future for a lady.

Rose protested and said that a number of ladies these days were earning their living.

'Not *ladies*,' said Lady Glensheil dismissively.

When they were joined by the gentlemen, the card tables were set up. Harry sat down with Lady Glensheil, Tristram and Sir Gerald and did not once look in Rose's direction.

Rose excused herself and followed by Daisy went up to her room. 'The captain is angry with me,' she said.

'You should maybe have told him,' ventured Daisy.

'I don't care what he thinks,' said Rose angrily.

Harry and the rest of them left for London the following morning. Harry went straight to his office and looked at the pile of mail waiting for him. He decided to employ another secretary. He drafted out an advertisement to appear in *The Lady* magazine and sent Becket off with it.

He felt guilty about Miss Jubbles. He should have noticed she had fallen in love with him. And he had told her all about Lady Rose working at the bank!

CHAPTER ELEVEN

When the Himalayan peasant meets the he-bear
  in his pride,
He shouts to scare the monster who will often
  turn aside.
But the she-bear thus accosted rends the peasant
  tooth and nail
For the female of the species is more deadly than
  the male.

Rudyard Kipling

Two weeks had passed since the return from Farthings, and Rose felt she had entered again into a type of luxurious convent. Once more she had to change at least six times a day and make calls with her mother or various ladies of society. She had to remember all the trivial things not to do, such as never opening a door herself, never looking round when she sat down – one had to assume a footman would be there to place the chair – and never to sit down on a chair still warm from a gentleman's bottom.

Daisy, too, was bored and restless. She tried to console herself by remembering the hard times in the business women's hostel. Now that it seemed as if Captain Harry was determined never to see Rose again, Daisy knew that meant she would not get a chance to see Becket.

The only freedom the pair had was when they were allowed go out on their bicycles in the park, and that was because the earl had taken the precaution of furnishing two of the footmen with bicycles and making sure they accompanied Rose and Daisy when they cycled.

And then, to make life really horrible, Tristram called and asked the earl's permission to pay his addresses and that permission was granted. Rose refused him again and was in deep disgrace.

Perhaps her parents would not have been so angry had they known that Rose had actually refused with a certain amount of reluctance this time. She was beginning to realize that the only hope of freedom for a lady of her class was to marry a complacent husband. She would have her own household. Her husband would presumably spend most of his time at his club or in the country killing things.

Daisy had told her about Harry's advertisement for a secretary and she wished he had asked her. He never called and he never attended any of the long, boring society events where she sat and fretted and counted the hours until she could return home to the sanctuary of books and privacy.

* * *

Harry was finding it hard to engage a suitable secretary. He did not want to make another mistake.

But at last he settled on a Miss Ailsa Bridge, daughter of Scottish missionaries. She was tall and thin with a long nose and pale hooded eyes. She was in her late thirties and had travelled extensively to the Far East with her parents to convert the heathen. Ailsa had excellent shorthand and typing. She came with a reference from Brigadier Bill Handy, who said that while she had been abroad she had provided the British government with useful intelligence about various situations in Burma.

She proved to be neat, efficient, and, above all, impersonal.

What he did not know because Ailsa did not consider it important enough to tell him was that two days after she had started work and while Harry was out of the office, she had sustained a visit from Miss Jubbles.

Miss Jubbles announced that she was the captain's former secretary and said that the china in the cupboard was her property. Armed in her new status of affianced lady, Miss Jubbles was ready to do battle, but Ailsa said mildly that she should go ahead and take her china.

'Very kind of you,' said Miss Jubbles gruffly. She had brought a box and tissue paper with her and she packed the china lovingly, glancing around occasionally at what she had considered to be her 'sanctum' for signs of change. There were new box files in different colours. The windows had been cleaned and sparkled in the late-spring sunlight. Other than that, it all looked heart-breakingly the same.

While she packed, Ailsa continued to type at great speed, keys rattling like a Gatling gun.

'Thank you,' said Miss Jubbles when she had finished. Ailsa raised her hands from the keys and put them in her lap. 'I'll be going, then.'

'Goodbye,' said Ailsa politely.

Miss Jubbles hefted up the box and paused in the doorway. 'Is the captain still running after that horrible creature, Lady Rose Summer?'

Ailsa's nose turned pink at the tip with annoyance. 'I do not know anything of Captain Cathcart's personal life, nor do I wish to do so.'

'Then you should. She's always in trouble and she'll get him killed one day.'

'If you are quite finished . . .' Ailsa's tone was frosty.

'Don't say I didn't warn you,' said Miss Jubbles.

When she had gone, Ailsa rose and went back to her room in a business women's hostel in South Kensington and collected a box of china she had brought from her parents' home in Scotland and had never used.

On her way back to Camden Town, Miss Jubbles comforted herself with the thought that Harry would notice the absence of his lovely rose-decorated cup.

The next time Ailsa served Harry tea in a cup embellished with lilacs, he did not notice the difference.

Rose would not admit it to herself but she was more determined than ever to find out the identity of the murderer as a way of seeing Harry again.

'I think perhaps I should encourage Tristram,' she said to Daisy.

'You're never thinking of marrying him!'

'No . . . although it has crossed my mind that I would not have so restricted a life were I married.'

'Then what happens if you fall in love? You're not the kind to have an affair.'

'I don't think I shall ever fall in love. Gentlemen are so . . . weird.'

'So why are you going to encourage that bleeder?'

'Language, Daisy!'

Daisy sighed. 'I mean, why?'

'Because he was Freddy's best friend. We know little of Freddy's habits or where he went apart from to these boring social affairs and to his club. He might have had a mistress and set her up in one of those places they set up mistresses, like St John's Wood, and the blackmailing stuff could be hidden there.'

'Why not tell the captain your idea? It's his job.'

Rose set her lips in a firm line. 'It is my idea and I will follow it through.'

In the weeks that followed, Harry had gone back to his usual detecting duties of finding lost dogs and covering up scandals. To his surprise, none of these scandals seemed to disturb his hard-working secretary. Miss Jubbles had smelt of rosewater. Ailsa smelled of peppermint, which seemed to be her only weakness.

Harry would have been amazed had he known that she despised society as heartily as Kerridge and admired her employer for having chosen to work for a living.

One day when Harry was out, Brigadier Billy Handy called. 'Came to see how you were settling in,' he said.

'Very well. Thank you for the recommendation.'

'Need to be discreet in this business. But you're used to that, hey?'

'Exactly,' said Ailsa.

'Mind you, it's funny work for a baron's son, albeit a younger one. He should find himself an heiress. Funny. I thought he and that beauty, Lady Rose, might have got hitched. No sign of that?'

'None whatsoever.'

When he had gone, Ailsa slid open the bottom drawer of her desk and took out a squat bottle of gin. She poured a strong measure into a teacup and knocked it back. She heard footsteps on the stairs and put the gin bottle away, took out a little bottle of peppermint essence and swallowed some, then darted to the cupboard and hid the teacup.

'I did not expect you back so soon, sir,' she said, as Harry limped in. It was one of his bad days and his leg was painful.

Harry paused at the door to the inner office. He sniffed the air. 'Funny, there's a smell of gin.'

'Brigadier Handy called when you were out. He wished to see how I was settling in,' said Ailsa.

'Really? I thought he was a brandy-and-soda man. Get me Lady Potterton's file, please.'

* * *

Harry decided to drop into his club that evening. It was simply called The Club and situated at the bottom of St James's. The first person he saw was the brigadier. He sank down in a chair opposite the old man and stretched out his throbbing leg.

'I believe you called at my office today,' said Harry.

'Yes, called round to see how Miss Bridge was settling in.'

'She is an excellent secretary. May I get you a drink? Gin and something?'

'Good heavens, man. I never touch the stuff.'

Harry laughed. 'My office smelt of gin. I thought you had left your scent behind.'

'Not me. And it can't be the missionaries' daughter. Must be one of those new cleaning materials. They smell a bit like gin. How are you, old man? I'll have a brandy and soda.'

'Nothing came of that murder case at Farthings or the murder of Freddy Pomfret. It really galls me to have a murder committed right under my nose.'

He signalled to the waiter and ordered two brandies and sodas.

'I read in the newspapers that Lady Rose was one of the guests,' said the brigadier. 'Good dowry there.'

'If I get married,' said Harry, 'it won't be to Lady Rose, neither will it be because of some female's dowry.'

'Oh, well, you haven't a chance anyway. I mean, with Lady Rose.'

'Why?'

'She's been seen about with Tristram Baker-Willis.'

'Nothing there. Lady Rose told me he had proposed marriage to her at Farthings and she had rejected him.'

'She might have changed her mind.'

'Why?'

'Those parents of hers keep a strong guard on her and I was talking to Hadshire the other day. Seems they really do want to ship her off to India. Now if she got married, well, Baker-Willis might prove a complacent husband and she'd get her freedom and her own household. Course she would need to provide the heir and the spare first.'

Harry had a sudden vision of Tristram in the throes of providing himself with an heir and experienced a shudder of revulsion.

After he had chatted about other things and left the club, Harry went back to his office and called the earl's residence. The earl's secretary, Matthew Jarvis, answered the phone. Harry asked if he might speak to Lady Rose.

'I am afraid,' said Matthew, 'that Lady Rose is not allowed to receive any phone calls.'

Disappointed, Harry rang off. He went to his secretary's desk and searched the drawers.

He smiled to himself. Nothing but a little bottle of peppermint cordial. The correct Miss Bridge probably did not drink any alcohol at all.

Tristram was driving Rose in Hyde Park the following day at the fashionable hour. Rose felt guilty as she stole glances at Tristram's radiant face. She began to have an uneasy feeling that the young man's motive in proposing to her had not been money after all.

'You must miss Mr Pomfret,' she said.

'Of course I do. We were great friends.'

'Did you know he was asking people for money?'

'No, but I can't say I blame him. I mean, quite low tradesmen are buying titles. So why not Freddy? It would have meant such a lot to him.'

Rose took the plunge. 'As you know, I think, he was blackmailing people.'

'He wouldn't do that.'

'Did he ever give you anything to keep for him? Documents? Anything like that?'

'The only thing he gave me was a box of cigars. He was trying to give up smoking and he loved cigars. Said if he kept them near him, he would smoke the lot in one day. He said he couldn't bear to give them away but to keep them in case he cracked and wanted one.'

'And did he?'

'What! No. Poor fellow was shot two days later. I say, look at that frightful hat.'

Harry reined in his horse under a tree and watched the couple. Rose looked very relaxed in a carriage dress of brown velvet trimmed with gold braid and with a dashing little hat tilted over her glossy brown curls.

Tristram was laughing and chatting. They seemed perfectly at ease with each other. He heard a voice from below him. 'Captain Cathcart!'

Now what bore was going to plague him on this awful, stupid day, he thought sourly. He looked down and saw Daisy.

He dismounted quickly. 'Why, Miss Levine. I have not seen you this age. What on earth is Lady Rose doing letting Mr Baker-Willis drive her around? I thought she had turned down a proposal of marriage from him.'

'She might come round,' said Daisy uneasily. 'I mean, she feels that if she got married and had her own place, and all, she wouldn't be such a prisoner. My lord and lady keep such a close watch on her. They're delighted she's going about with Mr Baker-Willis, so he got permission to drive her in the park. Mind you, she does say she wants to find out if Mr Pomfret told him anything or gave him anything to keep.'

'I wonder if she has found out anything,' said Harry. 'I tried to phone her but was told she was not allowed to accept calls.'

'We'll be cycling here in the morning at eight when its quiet. We're allowed to do that provided two footmen come with us. You could be there.'

'I'll be there,' said Harry.

He returned to Water Street and said to Becket, 'I'll give you some money to buy two bicycles for us.'

'Very good, sir.'

'I never asked you, Becket. Where did you learn to cycle?'

'When I was a boy, sir. Where did *you* learn to cycle?'

'In Africa.'

'That would be during the war.'

'So you had a cycle when you were a boy? I somehow thought your parents were poor.'

'Was it during the war, sir?'

'Becket, we should not stand here all day wasting time. You'd better get to the cycle shop as fast as possible.'

Becket went off, reflecting that the captain never liked to talk about the war, and left Harry wondering, not for the first time, why Becket was so cagey about his past.

Rose and Daisy headed for the park in the morning. It was a beautiful day, the twelfth of May, Saint Pancras Day, the patron saint of ice, because farmers believed that winter had a last blast around the beginning of the month. 'Shear your sheep in May,' they would say, 'and you won't have any sheep left to shear.' But the weather was golden, with a light morning mist drifting around the boles of the trees in the park.

Rose loved the park at this hour of the morning when there were so few people about, only a few footmen walking their owners' dogs.

They were cycling along the Broad Walk when Rose saw the familiar figures of Harry and Becket cycling towards them.

She and Daisy dismounted and waited for them to come up to them. 'Miss Levine told me you would be here,' said Harry.

Rose shot an accusing look at Daisy. 'I didn't tell you,' said Daisy, 'in case you wouldn't come.'

'I'm surprised you came at all,' said Rose to Harry. 'I thought you had taken a dislike to me.'

'Never mind that,' said Harry hurriedly. 'Daisy – I mean, Miss Levine – told me that you were going to ask Tristram if Freddy had asked him to keep something for him.'

'I did ask, but he said Freddy had only asked him to keep a box of cigars because Freddy was trying to give up smoking them but couldn't bear to give them away. He wanted Tristram to keep them for him in case he decided he couldn't hold off any longer. Nothing there.'

Harry stood in silence. He had taken off his cap and the breeze blew a heavy lock of hair over his forehead.

'I wonder,' he said. 'I wonder if there's anything other than cigars inside that box.'

'Wouldn't the police have found it?'

'Not necessarily. If it just looked like a box of cigars, they wouldn't waste time on it. I'm going to have a look.'

'How?' asked Rose. Daisy and Becket had walked a little way away, wheeling their bicycles. The earl's footmen lounged beside a tree.

'Simple. I'll pay a call on him and ask for a cigar.'

'If there is anything other than cigars in that box, how will I find out? If you call on me, you will probably be told I am not at home.'

'Can you slip out of the house?'

'It's difficult. The servants have been told to report my every move. These footmen will report my meeting you.'

'Do you have any social engagements for this evening?'

'No, thankfully. I am so weary of the round of balls and parties and calls.'

'Is the front door locked?'

'No, not until last thing at night.'

'As I remember,' said Harry, 'there is an ante-room off the hall. I will try to get in and wait there at, say, seven o'clock. I will call on Tristram at five. He will be getting dressed to go out, I should think, at that time. If you wait in that ante-room for me, I can tell you what I have found. But I fear it is going to prove to be a box of cigars and nothing else.'

Harry presented himself at Tristram's flat at five o'clock. A manservant told him that Mr Baker-Willis was asleep and did not want to be roused until six.

'It's all right,' said Harry airily. 'He must have forgotten he was expecting me. I'll wait.'

'In here, sir.'

He ushered Harry into a cluttered living-room. The room contained a horsehair sofa and two armchairs. Occasional tables were topped with ornaments, glass cases full of stuffed birds, photographs and waxed fruit. A table at the window was piled high with racing journals and copies of the *Pink 'Un*.

'May I fetch you some refreshment?' asked the manservant.

'No, no,' said Harry airily. 'Go about your business.'

'Very good, sir.'

Harry waited until the door had closed behind the servant and then began to search. He was just beginning to think that perhaps Tristram had taken the box to his bedroom when he suddenly saw a window-seat and went and lifted the lid. There on the top was the box of cigars. A box of Romeo Y Julietas, the cedar-wood box nailed shut and sealed with the familiar green-and-white label.

Harry felt disappointed. He would have nothing to report to Lady Rose. He was about to put it back when he noticed a thin slit along the label. He held it up to the light. Was it possible it had been opened and nailed shut again?

He tucked the box under his coat and made his way quietly out, lifting his card from the salver on the hall table and hoping the manservant would not remember his name.

He motored back to Water Street. 'I've got it,' he said to Becket. 'I think it's been opened already.'

'I'll get a chisel,' said Becket.

'No, perhaps we should leave it like this until we see the ladies. Then we can all examine it together.'

'If you will forgive me for saying so, sir, perhaps it would be better to open it here in case it contains items of an insalubrious nature.

'You're right. Bring the chisel.'

Harry waited impatiently until Becket returned. Then he slid the chisel under the lid and prised it open.

'By all that's holy, Becket,' he exclaimed. 'We've struck gold. What have we here?'

He lifted out four letters tied with pink silk ribbon. He untied the ribbons and started to read. The letters were addressed to Lord Alfred, passionate, yearning love letters describing their affair in detail and signed 'Your Loving Jimmy.'

'Dear me,' said Harry. 'I don't think the ladies

should see these. Very graphic. No wonder Lord Alfred paid up. What else have we? Photographs.'

One was a photograph of Lady Jerry in a passionate embrace with a young man in footman's livery. It looked as if it had been taken beside the Thames. The couple were lying on the grass, the remains of a picnic beside them.

There was only one more photograph. It was of Angela Stockton in an open-air restaurant, also by the river. Beside her a waiter was in the act of carving thin slices of roast beef, although Angela's plate was already piled high and the photographer had captured a look of anticipatory greed on her face.

'So our famous vegetarian, Becket, caught in the act.'

'It's not a crime,' said Becket.

'This would frighten her. She has set herself up to promote vegetarianism. People pay to join her society. She has even given lectures in America. It looks as if Mrs Jerry decided to go to the police and one of them killed her.'

'Are you going to take this to Kerridge?'

'No, let me think. They should be given a chance to explain themselves. What if the blackmailer is Tristram, who knew what was in the box and decided to make some money for himself?'

Rose and Daisy waited anxiously in the ante-room. Then they heard the front door open and the next moment Harry and Becket entered the room.

'You're a clever girl,' said Harry to Rose. 'The blackmailing stuff was in the box.'

'What is it?' asked Rose, reaching for the letters.

'No, don't read those,' said Harry sharply. 'They are letters to Lord Alfred from a young man with whom he had been having an affair. If the police got hold of these, he could go to prison and this Jimmy with him. You can look at the photographs.'

Rose exclaimed, 'Oh, do look at Mrs Stockton, Daisy. Positively salivating over roast beef. And Mrs Jerry! How disgusting. But our criminal must be Lord Alfred.'

'It could be Tristram,' said Harry. 'Have you thought of that?'

'Oh, dear, what are we going to do?'

'I will see Lord Alfred tomorrow.'

'And I will see Mrs Stockton,' said Rose.

'How can you get out of the house?'

'I will just go,' said Rose. 'I will be in trouble again.'

'Well, I cannot see Angela Stockton shooting and drugging and strangling over roast beef. But you are not to give her the photograph until she tells you who was blackmailing her. I believe someone knew the contents of this box and took over the blackmailing from Mr Pomfret.'

'And then do we go to the police?'

'If it should prove to be either Tristram or Lord Alfred, yes, certainly.'

'Kerridge will charge you with withholding vital evidence.'

'I believe Kerridge will be only too grateful to have the case cleared up.'

* * *

Rose hardly slept that night. What would Angela say? How would she react? The next morning she fretted that her mother would insist on her making calls and so she sent Daisy to say she had a headache. Lady Polly was feeling well disposed towards her daughter because she guessed that Rose was about to thaw and accept Tristram's hand in marriage and so she contented herself with telling Daisy to bathe her daughter's forehead in eau de cologne.

The countess went off to make her calls while her husband slept by the fire. At three in the afternoon, Rose and Daisy went quickly out of the house. The lady's maid, Turner, had promised not to tell anyone they had gone out without permission.

Rose and Daisy giggled over the forthcoming confrontation. It seemed hilarious to them that anyone would pay such a large sum to a blackmailer because they had been caught out eating roast beef.

As they approached Angela's house, Daisy suddenly burst into song:

Oh! The roast beef of England,
And old England's roast beef.

Rose burst out laughing and had to stop and mop her streaming eyes.

'Oh, Daisy,' she gasped, 'how are we ever going to get through this without laughing?'

'*She* won't find it funny,' said Daisy.

'No, she won't,' agreed Rose, suddenly sober.

'Here's her house. I'm suddenly beginning to wish she weren't at home.'

Angela's butler disappeared with their cards. Daisy was very proud to have her own case of visiting cards.

He reappeared and asked them to follow him to the drawing-room. Rose shivered. Although the day was warm, inside seemed to hold all the chill of winter.

Angela rose to meet them as they were ushered into the drawing-room. She was wearing a black-and-gold Turkish turban of a type favoured by ladies almost a hundred years ago. Her long loose gown was of deep purple velvet trimmed with gold embroidery.

'How very kind of you to call,' she fluted. Her American accent sounded peculiar because over the years Angela had tried to replace it with an upper-class English one, but her voice seemed to be permanently stuck somewhere in mid-Atlantic, neither one nor the other.

'Do be seated. I was about to have some fennel tea. May I press you to some?'

Daisy stifled a giggle, having had a sudden vision of both of them being pressed to a teapot.

'No, thank you,' said Rose. 'We are here on serious business.'

'Dear me. Nothing to do with that frightful business at Farthings?'

'Yes, it has.'

Angela got to her feet and went and closed the double doors of the drawing-room.

She returned and perched on the edge of a chair and looked at them inquiringly.

'A photograph has come into my possession,' said Rose, not feeling like laughing any more. 'I believe it was this photograph which Mr Pomfret was using to blackmail you.'

'Do you have this supposed photograph with you?'

'No,' said Rose. 'I left it at home.'

'Then why are you here? You cannot need money.'

'I need to know the name of the person who was blackmailing you. If you tell me that, I assure you I will destroy the photograph.'

'Why, it was Freddy Pomfret, the ghastly little counter jumper.'

'I think someone knew what the blackmailing material was and approached you at Farthings. I think Mrs Jerry threatened to go to the police and that was why she was murdered. Did you know why Mrs Jerry and Lord Alfred were being blackmailed as well?'

'Yes, Mr Pomfret took great delight in telling me.'

'So who approached you at Farthings?'

'It was Lord Alfred. Now, are you satisfied? Go and get that photograph.'

'Captain Cathcart is at present interviewing Lord Alfred. If Lord Alfred confesses, I will return the photograph.'

Angela clutched the arms on her chair so tightly that her knuckles stood out white.

'I am not going to have my life's work destroyed,' said Angela, staring straight ahead. She seemed almost to be talking to herself.

'I was brought up near Fairfax, Virginia. We were good family but we never had any money. Father

213

gambled and Mother kept telling me how plain I looked. And then I met Mr Stockton at a cotillion ball in Richmond. To my delight, he started courting me. I knew him to be very rich. He had clawed his way up from a poor family and thought that by marrying me it would give him class. He only survived a year of our marriage. The doctor diagnosed a heart attack.

'I came to London and set out to make myself known. I knew I was psychic and I had read the works of Mr Steiner. I set up my vegetarian society. I lectured all over Britain, and the States, too. I was someone at last.

'And then that Pomfret creature threatened to destroy me. Have you told the police?'

Rose shook her head.

'But your parents know about this.'

'No,' said Rose, 'they do not even know I am here.'

'Good, good, let me think.'

'There's nothing to think about,' said Rose sharply. 'As soon as I hear that Lord Alfred has confessed, you may have your photograph.'

Angela rose and paced the room, muttering, 'Must think, must think.'

Rose got to her feet as well. 'Now that you know the situation . . .' she was beginning when Angela strode to the book-shelves and lifted out an ugly-looking pistol and levelled it at Rose.

'Sit down,' she barked.

Rose and Daisy sank back in their chairs. Daisy remembered throwing herself in front of Rose last year to protect her from a bullet. Somehow, she didn't think she would ever have the courage to do that again.

'I detest flittery little débutantes like you, Lady Rose, smug in your own beauty, poking your nose into other people's business. That fool, Mrs Jerry, said that she couldn't take any more and was going to the police. I was not blackmailing her for money, but I wanted her to join my society and work for me. I lied and said I had my own photograph back but had kept the one of her. She laughed in my face. So I doctored that champagne and put it in her room and then strangled the old bitch while she lay unconscious.'

'So no one other than Freddy Pomfret was trying to blackmail you?'

'No.'

Rose moistened her dry white lips. 'So it was you who shot Freddy?'

'Yes, and I enjoyed doing it. I ransacked his flat but couldn't find anything. Where did you find it?'

'He had put the material in a cigar box and given it to Tristram Baker-Willis for safekeeping.'

Angela gave a harsh laugh. 'Amateurs, blundering greedy amateurs out to destroy my reputation. Do you know that the Duchess of Terford has just joined my society? A duchess!'

'Please do put down that gun,' said Rose, striving to keep her voice level.

'No, must think, think, think. Ah, you, Levine, you will go back and fetch that photograph and if you are not here with it after an hour, I will shoot your mistress.'

'I ain't leaving her!' said Daisy.

'Go, Daisy,' said Rose. 'You know what to do.'

Daisy looked at her for a long moment and then got up and hurried from the room.

Harry was seated in front of Lord Alfred. He slowly drew the bundle of letters from his pocket.

'How much?' demanded Lord Alfred.

'I am not here to blackmail you. In fact, if you can tell me one thing, I will give them to you.'

'What do you want to know?'

'Did you shoot Freddy Pomfret?'

'No, I swear on my life I didn't. I wanted to. I knew I would go to prison if those letters were ever made public.'

'How did he get hold of them?'

'I met a young artist called Jimmy Portal. He was not a very good artist but he was very beautiful. He pursued me and I was seduced. Then I was terrified of it coming out, knowing I would be sent to prison. I returned his letters. He waited for me outside The Club one evening. He thrust his letters at me and said I must keep them forever. I told him harshly that I wanted to have no more to do with him. Pomfret told me afterwards that he had witnessed the scene from the window of The Club. He saw me hurrying off and saw Jimmy throwing the letters in the gutter. He nipped out and got them.

'He bragged that it was the letters that gave him the idea of being a blackmailer. He was a keen amateur photographer and said he had compromising pictures of Mrs Jerry and Mrs Stockton. He said he had just realized a way of getting money to buy a title. I paid. Of course I paid.

'Then when I went to Farthings and saw you there along with Mrs Stockton and Mrs Jerry, I was afraid.'

'Did anyone else try to blackmail you while you were at Farthings?'

'Yes. Mrs Stockton whispered that she had destroyed the photograph of her but had kept the letters. She said I must work for her society and travel with her. Then she told me that Mrs Jerry was going to go to the police. I was prepared to flee the country, but then she died. I knew Mrs Stockton had probably done it, but what could I do? You know what happens to fellows like me in prison.'

Harry felt a spasm of dread. Lord Alfred's voice held the ring of truth.

He had sent Rose blithely off to see Angela Stockton, and Angela was a murderess.

'Excuse me.' Harry got to his feet and rushed from the room.

Lord Alfred looked at the letters lying on the table. He picked them up and took them to the fireplace. He took out a silver box of vestas and struck one and held it to the edge of the packet until a flame took hold and then he threw the burning packet into the fireplace.

He sat down again and covered his face with his hands and wept.

CHAPTER TWELVE

*Really, if the lower orders don't set us a good
example, what on earth is the use of them?*

Oscar Wilde

Rose felt sick. Angela's eyes were glittering with a
mad light, but the hand holding the gun never
wavered. Rose tried to think coolly and calmly but
jumbled thoughts raced through her brain. That
famous line from adventure stories she had read –
'With one bound he was free' – tumbled into her brain.
Would Daisy bring the photograph or would she find
Captain Cathcart and get help? Her mother had
insisted she go back to wearing 'proper stays' and a
steel had edged itself loose and was cutting into her.
The whalebone stiffening in the high collar of her
gown was digging into her neck. If she had accepted
Tristram's proposal and settled for an uneventful
married life, she would never have landed in this mess.

'If you shoot me,' said Rose, finding her voice, 'how
do you expect to get away with it?'

'I will leave the country and hide abroad. They will never find me.'

'If you have to leave the country, Mrs Stockton, what is the point of wanting the photograph? Your reputation will be ruined by this mad action of yours.'

'*I am not mad!*'

Rose was aware of the bell-rope next to her chair. If only she could tug it, a servant would appear, and surely this whole household of servants wasn't party to the murders.

'What happened to Murphy? What happened to Mr Pomfret's manservant? Did you kill him, too?'

'I paid him to leave for Ireland. He was glad to accept. He didn't know I'd killed Pomfret but I didn't want him in that flat in case he found that photograph. I said I was looking after him out of kindness and to honour Pomfret's memory.'

Rose put her hand to her forehead and swayed in her chair. 'I feel faint,' she said.

'Then faint,' snapped Angela.

Rose swayed in her chair nearer the bell-rope. Then, as if about to lose her balance, she seized the bell-rope.

The double doors of the drawing-room opened and a footman stared at the tableau and then retreated. Rose could hear him running down the stairs.

To her amazement, Angela, in her fixed concentration, had not even noticed.

But suddenly a voice shouted from downstairs, 'We've got to get the police!'

Angela's eyes widened and her finger tightened on the trigger.

Rose threw herself to one side, tipping her chair over onto the floor, just as the gun went off with a deafening report. The recoil jerked Angela backwards and she gave a howl of pain and dropped the gun.

Rose sprang up from the floor. She fell on Angela, screaming and clawing and biting, dragging her out of her chair while Angela fought to get the gun. Angela was wiry and strong. She rolled Rose under her and her bony hands encrusted with rings fastened around Rose's throat.

And then Harry erupted into the room, followed by Becket and Daisy. They had met Daisy in the street as she was running to get help.

Harry seized Angela by her thin shoulders and jerked her off Rose. He turned and addressed the gawping servants clustered in the doorway. 'Fetch something to tie her up!'

'No,' gasped Angela. 'I am calm now. I will go quietly.'

Two policemen came into the room. 'Arrest this woman for murder and phone Detective Superintendent Kerridge. We will follow you to the police station and make statements,' ordered Harry.

Angela stood up and with a quaint dignity said, 'I must take my medicine with me. I have a bad heart.'

'Send a servant.'

'No, I have it here, over in that desk.'

She went to the desk and took out a small bottle. She squared her shoulders. 'Now, I am ready.'

Rose looked wildly at Harry but he stared back at her, his face a mask. The two policemen moved forward. 'If you will come with us . . .' one started to say. Angela twisted the cork off the bottle and tipped the contents down her throat.

'In a moment,' she gasped. Her face contorted and she clutched her neck. Then she held her stomach and moaned as she sank to the floor.

'She's taken poison,' said Harry. He turned to the servants. 'Send for a doctor. Miss Levine, take Lady Rose into another room, for God's sake. Lady Rose, there is blood on your dress. Are you wounded?'

'One of the steels in my stays came loose,' said Rose with a hysterical laugh. 'You knew she was going to poison herself, didn't you?'

'You are upset and don't know what you are saying. We will talk later.'

By the time Kerridge lumbered up the stairs, Angela Stockton was dead. He had taken half an hour to arrive, and in that half-hour Harry, Becket, Rose and Daisy had a hurried consultation to get their stories right.

'I want to know what you have all been up to,' said Kerridge. The four had retreated to a morning-room on the same floor.

'Lady Rose is still shocked,' began Harry. 'Mrs Stockton held a gun on her and was going to shoot her. Miss Levine managed to escape and came to look for me. Fortunately we saw her on the street and came here immediately.'

Kerridge turned his grey gaze on Rose. 'Why was Mrs Stockton trying to kill you?'

'I had been thinking and thinking about the

murders,' said Rose in a low voice. 'I thought she might have committed them. I always thought she was mad. I came with Miss Levine and challenged her. She pulled out a gun and said she was going to shoot me. She confessed to both murders. She said she shot Mr Pomfret because he was blackmailing her. He had a photograph of her eating roast beef.'

Kerridge's bushy eyebrows nearly vanished into his hairline. 'Do you mean she killed twice over a plate of roast beef?'

'She said she had built up a world-wide reputation as a vegetarian. She said Mrs Jerry was going to the police. She said Mr Pomfret had a picture of her in a compromising position with a young footman. Although she did not have the evidence, Mrs Jerry thought she had.'

'And what was Lord Alfred being blackmailed about?'

'I believe it was because he had got a servant girl pregnant and she died in childbirth,' said Harry smoothly. 'We only have what Mrs Stockton told Lady Rose. There is no proof of that.'

'The press are going to have a field day with this,' said Kerridge.

'I think it would be better,' said Harry, 'if we stick to the roast beef blackmail. We cannot mention the other two because there is no evidence.'

'At least Mrs Stockton saved us a court case. Did you not guess she was going to poison herself?'

'How could I?' said Harry. 'She said it was heart medicine.'

'I don't believe you. There's a lot in your statements I don't believe. But I'm very glad to have two murders solved.'

'May we please leave further questioning until tomorrow?' asked Harry. 'Lady Rose has been through the most terrible ordeal.'

'Very well. But Lady Rose, you did a mad and foolish thing. If you had any suspicions that the killer was Mrs Stockton, then you should have come to me. Never do anything like that again. Go back to your society life. Get married. Have children. That's what a woman is supposed to do.'

'You are just an old-fashioned fuddy-duddy, Mr Kerridge,' said Rose. 'Women should be independent and have the vote.'

'Those trouble-making suffragettes should all be locked up. I want you all at Scotland Yard first thing in the morning.'

Rose, Harry, Becket and Daisy emerged from Angela's house. The day had turned dark and they were nearly blinded by the magnesium flashes of the press on the doorstep going off in their faces.

'This is bad,' said Rose as they drove off. 'My parents are never going to forgive me. Why did you not tell Kerridge the truth about why Lord Alfred was being blackmailed?'

Harry shrugged. 'He did not murder anyone. It would extend the inquiry and I am heartily tired of the whole thing.'

* * *

The Roast Beef Murders hit the papers the following morning. Photographs of Rose, looking beautiful, stared out wide-eyed from every newspaper. She was hailed as a heroine, as the New Woman of this new century.

Rose's parents recovered from their initial fury to bask in the reflected glory of their daughter's bravery. Invitations poured into the earl's town house, every society hostess wanting to brag that she had managed to get the latest celebrity to attend her ball or dinner.

Rose became tired of relating the edited version she had told Kerridge over and over again.

Tristram seemed to be always at her side, saying loudly that he should have been there to protect her.

Rose came to the conclusion that nothing could make her want to marry such a boring man as Tristram. She decided she had better get rid of him. Everyone seemed to assume that an engagement was in the offing.

He was driving her in the park one day a few weeks later. Rose was in low spirits. Harry had not called or sent any message.

'I am thinking of joining the suffragette movement,' she said, unfurling her lace parasol to shield her face from the rays of the sun.

'Eh, what? You're joking, of course.'

'Not in the slightest. If I marry, I would expect my husband to attend rallies with me.'

Tristram was so shocked and alarmed that he

blurted out, 'Any husband worth his salt would give you a good beating first.'

'Take me home now,' ordered Rose.

The former Miss Jubbles, now the new Mrs Jones, left church that day on the arm of the baker. She had experienced savage pangs of jealousy when she read about the exploits of what she considered her 'old rival' in the newspapers. But now she felt simply proud to be a married lady.

She had inherited a comfortable sum of money on her mother's death, and as Mr Jones drove her off in their new motor car under the admiring gaze of the neighbours, she felt she would burst with pride.

Her replacement, Ailsa Bridge, filed Harry's cases, typed his letters and occasionally fortified herself with gin. She no longer kept a bottle in her desk drawer but had a flask of gin firmly anchored by one garter under her skirts.

Harry was plucking up courage to try to call on Rose. It was only his duty, he told himself. He at last presented himself at the earl's mansion to be told that Lady Rose was not at home. This he translated that she was not being allowed to see him.

Rose was, in fact, upstairs in the drawing-room being confronted by her parents. 'It's no use your protesting, my girl,' the earl was saying. 'It's India for you. And don't threaten me with that business of me stopping the king visiting. It would harm you as much as me,

225

and that precious Captain Cathcart would go to prison. The season's nearly at an end. You've led us all to think that you might accept Baker-Willis after all and then you tell us some story that he had threatened to beat you, which I don't believe. Should have beaten you myself.

'I will arrange for you to sail at the end of the summer. You may take Levine with you, but you'll be staying with the Hulberts, remember them?'

'I do. Mrs Hulbert is a cross, overbearing woman.'

'Enough of that. Need someone to keep an eye on you. Get yourself a nice officer. No adventurers, mind.'

Inspector Judd said to his superior, 'You never quite believed Lady Rose's story, did you, sir?'

'No, I did not. Oh, yes, the Stockton woman did commit the murders, but I think either Lady Rose or Cathcart found the blackmailing stuff. I think they're protecting Lord Alfred.'

'Why?'

'Because that young man had an affair with another man, I'm sure of that. I just *sense* it.'

'But that should have been reported!'

'I let it go because we got our murderer and we've enough on our plate without hounding Lord Alfred. But I do think that somehow Lady Rose or Captain Cathcart decided to take the law into their own hands. I don't like it. Let's just hope Lady Rose settles down and gets married. I'm sure she's the one who causes all the trouble. Women always do.'

226

The superintendent did not see the paradox in that in his dreams of the revolution, there were always beautiful women on the barricades beside him, armed to the teeth and waving the red flag.

'What am I to do?' wailed Rose later that day. 'I don't want to go to India and sit in the heat while the memsahibs gossip about me.'

Daisy bit her thumb and looked at her sideways. 'If I were you, I'd go to the captain for help.'

'What can he do?'

'I don't know,' fretted Daisy. 'But it's his job to fix things for people.'

'How are we to get there? You know I am guarded.'

'Same as last time,' said Daisy cheerfully. 'You're in such disgrace that another disgrace won't matter. Your parents are very wealthy. And yet they go on the whole time about the money they've wasted on you.'

'That is their way. They all go on like that. It's a way of blackmailing their daughters into getting married during their first season. Most of the poor girls take anyone who offers.'

'Let's just go,' said Daisy eagerly.

'I would rather slip out of the house when they do not know I have gone. Have we any engagement for this evening?'

'Not that I know of.'

'Then after dinner, I will say they have upset me and I wish to go to my room and read. Then we will go out and get a hansom to take us to Water Street. What would I do without you, Daisy?'

'I did call, you know,' said Harry when they were all settled in his front parlour. 'I was told you were not at home. Are you feeling better, Lady Rose? Got over the shock?'

'I get a few nightmares,' said Rose.

Harry had the unkind thought that Lady Rose seemed to be quite up to saving herself. He felt he should have been the one to get the gun away from Angela Stockton.

'Miss Levine suggested I should come to you for advice, that being your job,' said Rose.

'Have you lost something? Servants been stealing from you?'

Daisy bristled. 'Not with me around.'

'It's just that my parents are now determined to ship me off to India. They have suggested that before and I always threatened to tell people about Father hiring you to deter the king from visiting.

'Well, that won't work any more because they point out that if I did, you would be arrested. So I have come to ask you to think of something else.'

Harry sat silently for a long moment. Then he said, 'The trouble is that I do not think they will ever give up until you are married.'

'I've got it!' Daisy clapped her hands, her eyes shining. 'Why don't you marry my lady, Captain Cathcart?'

'Don't be cheeky, Daisy,' admonished Rose.

'Perhaps there is a way out,' said Harry slowly. 'If I proposed marriage to you and suggested a long engagement, that would give you time. Then, after a year, you can break off the engagement, but during that year, as I shall be busy with my work, you will find time to find someone suitable.'

'My parents would never let me accept,' said Rose, a high colour on her cheeks. Did the captain need to look at her in that measuring way, as if she were nothing more than a business proposition?

'I think they would. I am of good family. I can afford to pay the no doubt horrendous marriage settlements that their lawyers will insist upon. I can be very persuasive. They will be anxious to see you settled.'

'You would need to look . . . affectionate,' said Rose.

'Oh, I can manage that.'

'Go on, Rose,' urged Daisy. 'It's him or India. Think of the heat, the flies, the boozy officers, the bitchy memsahibs, and what about the Hulberts?'

'Who are the Hulberts?' asked Harry.

'Some terrible dragon of a woman who is an old friend of Mama's,' said Rose. 'What if I take a fancy to some gentleman shortly after this supposed engagement?'

'Then you terminate the engagement early,' said Harry cheerfully. 'Your parents won't mind so long as you have someone, anyone, to marry.'

Rose was beginning to find all this humiliating. Harry could at least have shown a little warmth instead of looking at her as if she were nothing more than another case.

'I'm sure I can think of something else,' she said stiffly. 'Goodbye, Captain Cathcart.'

'No, stay,' he said quickly. 'I have hurt your feelings by being so detached about it all.' He suddenly smiled at her, that smile of his which softened the harsh lines of his handsome face. 'And it would serve your purpose, would it not?'

'May I say something, sir?' interposed Becket, who was standing behind Harry's chair.

'By all means, Becket. Pray be seated.'

Becket sat down next to Daisy. 'Lady Rose,' he said, 'I gather you have led a particularly restricted life of late. Were you engaged to my master, you would have more freedom. Captain Cathcart works hard, but I am sure he would be prepared to attend social events with you. You would not be the target any more of men you did not like, nor would you be so closely guarded by your parents. I think it is a very good idea.'

'Oh, very well,' said Rose ungraciously. 'When do you plan to approach my parents?'

'Late tomorrow morning.'

'I do not think for a moment you will have any success,' said Rose, 'but thank you for trying. Daisy, are you ready?'

'Well, I think it downright noble of him,' said Daisy on the road back. 'You would be able to help him with his detecting like you once wanted to.'

'I have had enough of horrors and frights to last me a lifetime,' snapped Rose, huffily thinking that

Captain Cathcart might have said something like how honoured he was, or that he would do anything in the world to help her.

To Rose's relief, after stopping the hansom on the far corner of the square and walking the rest of the way on foot, they were able to slip in unnoticed.

She finally fell asleep that night torn between worrying thoughts that her parents might not accept the captain's proposal and being uneasily afraid that they might.

The following morning, the earl looked up from his newspaper as Brum, the butler, entered the morning-room and said Captain Cathcart had called.

'What does that man want now?' demanded the countess. 'You didn't send for him, did you?'

'No, but I'd better see him. Useful chap. Put him in the study, Brum.'

'Very good, my lord.'

The earl entered his study and blinked at the vision that was Captain Harry Cathcart. The captain was wearing an impeccably tailored morning suit. His thick black hair with only a trace of grey at the temples was brushed and pomaded until it shone.

'Ah, Cathcart,' said the earl. 'What's amiss?'

'I am glad to say that nothing is amiss,' said Harry pleasantly. 'I have come to ask for your daughter's hand in marriage.'

The earl sank down into a battered leather armchair. 'This is a shock. I must say I admire your cheek. Won't do, you know. You're a tradesman.'

'I am of good family, as you know,' said Harry, 'and I can now afford to keep your daughter in style.'

'But you are one of society's misfits!'

'As is your daughter. My lord, think calmly about my proposal. Can you envisage your daughter married to a conventional man? Lady Rose would quickly become bored and go looking for trouble.'

The earl took out a large handkerchief and mopped his brow. 'This is so sudden,' he said like the heroine of a romance. 'I don't know what my wife's going to say to all this.'

'Why don't we ask her?'

'Follow me. But she'll say the same thing.'

Harry followed the earl to the morning-room. Lady Polly was sitting reading her husband's newspaper at a table strewn with the remains of a hearty breakfast.

'That's mine!' said the earl, snatching the paper from her. 'You know I don't like anyone reading it until I've finished with it. You've crumpled it.' He turned to an attendant footman. 'Take this away and iron it again.' Newspapers were always ironed so that nasty black ink should not sully aristocratic fingers.

'Captain Cathcart,' said Lady Polly. 'Have you breakfasted?'

'Thank you, yes.'

'Coffee? Tea?'

'Coffee, if you please.'

Another liveried footman went to the sideboard to get Harry's coffee. When it was placed in front of him, the earl said to the footman, 'Take yourself off and stand outside the door and make sure no one comes in. Got private business.'

Lady Polly looked at her husband in amazement. When the servant had left, she asked, 'What is going on? Not more skulduggery, I hope.'

'Worse than that,' said her husband. 'Cathcart here wants to marry Rose.'

'Well, the simple answer is no,' said Lady Polly placidly. 'You should have known better, Captain. A man in your position can hardly hope to be allowed to marry an heiress.'

'Then what will happen to Lady Rose?' asked Harry.

'We are sending her to India.'

'Is that such a good idea? What if there is another mutiny? What if she meets some adventurer who is only after her money?'

'Rose will be staying with a very good friend of mine who will look out for her,' said Lady Polly.

'A Mrs Hulbert, I believe?'

'Yes, how did you know that?' Lady Polly's eyes narrowed. 'Have you been seeing my daughter behind my back? Oh, dear God, do you *have* to marry her?'

'Nothing like that. Servants will gossip, you know.'

'No, I wouldn't know that, young man. Only very low people listen to servants' gossip.'

'This Mrs Hulbert has daughters of her own, has she not?'

'Yes, two. Bertha and Caroline.'

'I assume they didn't take at the season?'

'No, that's why they're going.'

'My lady, as I have heard,' said Harry, who had done his homework, 'the Hulbert daughters are singularly plain and of a somewhat sharp-natured temperament. You are foisting onto Mrs Hulbert a beautiful girl. Lady Rose will have a horrible time. Mrs Hulbert will make no push to have Lady Rose settled until she has seen her own daughters safely engaged. She may even keep Lady Rose in the background. Do you dislike your own daughter so much that you must needs guard her night and day and possibly try to force her into an unsuitable marriage? Remember that she is now capable of working for a living, and as soon as she reaches her majority, she may simply leave home to get away from the pressure.

'I doubt if she will ever forgive you for putting her in asylum.'

'We didn't know it was an asylum. She just thought it was a nerve place where she could be talked out of her odd ideas,' said the earl.

'You are in danger of forfeiting the love of your daughter,' pursued Harry.

'Don't be vulgar,' said Lady Polly. Really, what was this odd man talking about? Daughters simply did as they were told. Everyone knew that. Did he expect her to behave like some common character in a cheap play?

'We'll be here all day,' grumbled the earl. 'Where's that newspaper?'

'You told the servants not to interrupt us,' his wife reminded him.

A look of cunning came into the earl's usually guileless eyes. 'Wait in the drawing-room, Cathcart.'

When the door closed behind Harry, the earl said, 'We needn't bother. Let the man make his proposal. Rose isn't going to accept him.'

The worry cleared from Lady Polly's face.

'Of course. I'll go and get Rose.'

Rose was waiting in her sitting-room. She was dressed in a blue organdie gown with a little white spot. Blue kid shoes were on her feet and blue ribbons were threaded in her thick hair.

'You look very fine!' exclaimed her mother. 'Were we due to go out anywhere?'

'No, Mama.'

'You're to go down to the drawing-room. Captain Cathcart wishes to propose marriage to you.' She gave a chuckle. 'Hurry along then. You've got ten minutes to deal with him.'

Rose entered the drawing-room and a footman closed the double doors behind her.

The couple studied each other for a moment, each reflecting how fine the other one looked.

Harry walked forward and took Rose by the hand. Then he sank down on one knee. 'Lady Rose,' he said huskily, 'would you do me the very great honour of giving me your hand in marriage?'

'There's no need to play-act,' said Rose.

'Who knows when they'll walk in on us?'

'All right. Yes, I do.'

Harry stood up and fished in his pocket and drew out a little box. He opened it to reveal a sapphire-and-diamond ring.

'Oh, how beautiful,' said Rose, as he slid it on her finger. 'You should not have gone to so much trouble.'

'He gone yet?' asked the earl.

Lady Polly looked down from the window. 'His motor car is still there with his manservant at the wheel.'

'I think we'd better see what's going on.' The earl sighed and put down his freshly ironed paper with reluctance.

'They're coming,' said Harry, cocking his head to one side. He drew Rose into his arms.

'You're not going to kiss me, are you?' demanded Rose, blushing.

'No, just lean your head on my manly chest.'

The doors opened and the earl and countess stood stricken at the tableau in front of them.

'Congratulate me,' said Harry. 'I am the happiest of men.'

There was nothing that Rose's parents could do now but give their blessing.

When Harry had gone, the countess rounded on her daughter. 'Not a word out of you. You have thrown yourself away. Come, dear, I need a cup of tea.'

The earl went back to the morning-room and picked up his precious newspaper only to find it had fallen in the marmalade dish. 'You,' he said to a footman, 'take this away and clean it and iron it again!'

Dr McWhirter's corpse – or what was left of it – was eventually discovered by a gamekeeper. Foxes and other predators had done their busy work and left the rest to the maggots. The bullet had dropped down through the exposed skeleton and fallen to the ground. When two policemen came to remove the remains, one large regulation boot ground the bullet down into the forest floor. From the rags still clinging to the skeleton, they assumed it to be the remains of some tramp.

The remains were buried in a pauper's grave. Foul play was not suspected.

Superintendent Kerridge read of Harry's engagement in the *Times*. He was happy for both of them and assumed they would settle down to a conventional married life. He doubted if he would ever see them again and felt a tinge of sadness. He had felt comfortable in their company because he sensed the three of them in their way did not really fit in anywhere and that had forged a bond between them.

He had received news that Peregrine Stockton was back in the country. It crossed his mind that he ought to warn Lady Rose and then decided against it. After all, the man had had an unfortunate mother and there were no charges against him.

Miss Ailsa Bridge ferreted through her belongings, some of which were still in boxes, and found a crystal butter dish which she considered would do very well for an engagement present. Then she took another sip of gin.

* * *

Lady Polly had thawed somewhat towards the engagement. Harry had helped so many people in society that she found her daughter was regarded as fortunate. So it was with a lighter heart that she set out one sunny day to attend at garden party at Mrs Barrington-Bruce's home in Kensington accompanied by Rose and Daisy. Harry had promised to be there.

Luncheon was served at tables in the garden. Rose was not seated next to Harry, a good hostess having assumed that engaged couples saw enough of each other.

She had a guards' officer on one side and an elderly gentleman on the other, neither of whom seemed to wish to make conversation.

Harry was in conversation with a very pretty lady of mature years. The tops of her swelling white bosoms rose above a gown of midnight-blue moire. She was wearing a dashing little hat tipped over her glossy blonde curls. Harry was laughing at something she was saying. Rose reflected sourly that she had never seen Harry look so relaxed or happy before.

The guardsman next to her – what was his name again? She peered at the place card in front of him. Ah, Major Devery, that was it.

The major was crunching an ortolan, bones and all. She waited impatiently until he had finished and said, 'Who is that lady next to Captain Cathcart?'

'Eh, beg your pardon?'

One monocled eye swivelled in Rose's direction.

She repeated the question. The major stared down the table and then let out a guffaw. 'That's Mrs Winston. We call her the Merry Widow. Great flirt.'

A little black knot of jealousy tightened in Rose's stomach. Harry was her fiancé. He had no right to be so flagrantly enjoying the attentions of that blowsy creature whose hair was probably dyed.

The bit of the table she was seated at was in full sunlight. Her hat of fine straw did little to protect her head from the heat of the sun's rays. She suffered until the end of the luncheon and then with a muttered excuse got to her feet. Rose escaped to a shady part of the garden and sat down in an arbour. There was a slight breeze and the arbour was cool. She decided to sit for a few more minutes before rejoining the party.

Then she became aware of someone standing in front of her. She looked up.

Peregrine Stockton stood glaring down at her.

'Why, Mr Stockton,' said Rose. 'I was just about to go back to the party. It was so very hot at luncheon.'

'It was all your fault,' said Peregrine passionately. 'My poor mother would never have killed anyone had she not been blackmailed, and no one would have found out except for you and your nasty prying ways. You're like all these cold little virgins. A good roll in the hay is what you need.'

He smelt strongly of drink.

Rose got up and tried to go round him but he seized her and began to drag her towards some thick shrubbery. She opened her mouth to scream, but a hand was clamped over her mouth.

'Such a drama about Mrs Stockton,' Mrs Winston was saying as she walked with Harry from the lunch table.

'I'm only glad it's over,' said Harry, looking around for Rose. 'I believe her son left the country.'

'Oh, he's back, and I think he is as odd as his mother. I saw him peering out of the bushes while we were eating.' She had both hands clasped round Harry's arm.

He broke free and demanded harshly, 'Where? Where did you see him?'

Mrs Winston pointed. 'Over there.'

Harry strode off and left her standing looking after him.

Rose was lying in the bushes under Peregrine's weight and fighting like a tigress. One of his hands was fumbling under her dress as he was cursing about the amount of underclothes while the other hand was still clamped over her mouth. In frantic despair, she bit savagely down on the hand covering her mouth and Peregrine snatched it away with a howl of pain.

Rose screamed, 'Help!' at the top of her voice.

The next thing she knew was that Peregrine was jerked off her. Harry stood there, his eyes blazing. 'Get along,' he said to Rose, 'and don't say a word to anyone.'

'But he should be charged. He tried to rape me!'

'Don't say one damn word . . . please.'

He helped Rose to her feet. She smoothed down her dress and picked up her hat, which had fallen off.

Peregrine stood swaying, a leer on his face. 'She was begging for it.'

Harry drew back his fist and struck Peregrine full on the mouth.

As Peregrine fell, he turned and saw Rose still standing there. 'Go away!' he roared.

Rose emerged from the shrubbery and made her way back to the party. Daisy came up to her. 'You're as white as sheet, and your gown is torn at the hem.'

'Get me into the house, Daisy,' urged Rose, 'and then fetch some sewing materials and get me some brandy. I'll tell you about it later.'

Harry rejoined the party half an hour later and sought out his hostess. 'Have you seen my fiancée?' he asked.

'Yes, poor Lady Rose is in the library with her companion. She had a fainting fit in the gardens and tore her gown.'

'Where is the library?'

'Second door on the right off the hall.'

Harry walked into the library and jerked his head at Daisy. 'Leave us alone for a bit. Where's Lady Polly?'

'Gone for a nap. Her ladyship always likes to lie down after luncheon and so she asked Mrs Barrington-Bruce for the use of one of the bedrooms.'

'Good. We'll be out shortly.'

Rose had regained some colour. Daisy had mended the tear in her gown, bathed her temples with eau de cologne and poured her a stiff measure of brandy.

Rose was sitting bolt upright in a chair by the open window. Through the window came strains of music from the band of the Life Guards playing selections from *The Pirates of Penzance*.

'Why did you not call the police?' asked Rose.

He pulled up a chair and sat opposite her and took

her hand in his. 'Because it's a wicked world. Do you know what they say about women who have been raped, and I mean the police as well?'

Rose shook her head.

'They say, she was asking for it. The story would go round the clubs and your virginity would be in question. I have thrashed him soundly and I have told him I will kill him if he approaches you again.'

'I think men are animals,' said Rose, her voice breaking on a sob.

'Not all of us,' said Harry.

She snatched her hand away.

'You were flirting with that common widow.'

'Mrs Winston was flirting with me.'

'From where I was sitting, I could see you were definitely flirting.'

'I am engaged to you, not Mrs Winston.'

'Then kindly remember it.'

Harry was suddenly very angry.

'Is this all the thanks I get for having saved you? I am glad, repeat glad, that this is an engagement in name only because I would hate to be shackled to an ungrateful little shrew like you.'

He stalked out of the room.

Rose sat there for a long time. She finally decided that the least she could do was go to Harry and thank him. He should have realized she had only said these things because she was overset.

As she left the library, she was joined by her mother in the hall. 'I had such a good nap, dear,' said Lady Polly.

They walked outside together. A marquee had been erected for dancing. They entered the marquee. It was a splendid affair, having been laid with a French chalked floor and decorated with banks of flowers.

Harry Cathcart was dancing a lively polka with Mrs Winston. She was laughing up at him. Harry's bad leg did not seem to be troubling him at all.

Lady Polly looked from Harry to her daughter's set face. Really, she thought, we might be rid of him after all. Not that he isn't a good man. But trade! Our name should not be allied with trade.

Kerridge mopped his brow and made a mental note to tell his wife not to put too much starch in his collars. The window of his office was wide open but seemed to let nothing else in but brassy heat and the smell of drains and horse manure.

Inspector Judd came in and put a cup of tea on his boss's desk. 'Thought you could do with that, sir.'

'Ta. Sit down. I was really thinking of nipping round to the pub for a tankard of beer.'

'Quiet day. You should be able to manage it, sir. You remember that thieving pair of servants at Lady Glensheil's?'

'Yes. Any word of them?'

'No, disappeared into thin air. I was thinking of them only today, wondering how they'd managed to escape with all the police looking for them. Maybe we should have checked the ports.'

'Waste of manpower. That sort never leave the country. They just sink down into some thieves' kitchen. They'll be caught sooner or later, mark my words,' said Kerridge. 'That sort always get found out.'

Alice Turvey and the pot-boy, Bert Harvey, had bought a little shop in Brooklyn. The chef at Lady Glensheil's had taught Alice one day how to make meat pies with a light golden crust. They called their pie shop A Bit of England and built up a steady trade. They soon had enough money to buy false papers. They took the names of Mr and Mrs Kerridge.

Bert was already thinking of training up a cook and opening another shop.

They were regular attenders at St Anne's Episcopal church in Montagu Street and were regarded as pillars of the community by the other tradesmen.

Lady Rose went to Deauville with her parents and then on to Biarritz. Harry stayed in London. She did not write to him or answer any of his letters.

On their return, Daisy surprised Rose by asking for an evening off.

'You're not going to get into any more trouble, are you?' asked Rose anxiously.

'No, I just want to be by myself for a bit.'

Becket surprised Harry by asking for an evening off. He readily granted it but could not remember Becket ever before asking for any time off.

Becket and Daisy met in Hyde Park. It was quiet in the evening, with only a few couples strolling about.

'They're not going to get married, you know,' said Daisy gloomily. She and Becket had never spoken of marrying each other, and yet between them there was an understanding that they would be free to do so only if Rose married Harry.

'Perhaps there might be another murder to bring them together,' said Becket. 'Let's forget them and let me take you out for a nice supper. What would you like? I've been saving up. Champagne? Oysters?'

'Jellied eels,' said Daisy dreamily. 'I would love some jellied eels.'

'Then jellied eels it is!'

Also in this series

After a brief and ill-advised dalliance with the Suffragette movement, Lady Rose Summer's debut season in London society turns out to be a complete disaster. Rose's father suspects that her fiancé, Sir Geoffrey Blandon, is a first-class scoundrel and calls in Captain Harry Cathcart to investigate.

But when a malicious guest is found dead in suspicious circumstances, Rose becomes far more interested in discovering the truth than in landing a more appropriate suitor. As Harry and Rose begin to unravel a web of lies and rumour, a clever murderer sets out to make Rose's dreadful first season her last.

'Fans of the author's Agatha Raisin and Hamish Macbeth series should welcome this tale of aristocrats, house parties, servants, and murder.'
Publishers Weekly

To order your copies of other books in this
series, simply contact The Book Service (TBS)
by phone, email or by post. Alternatively visit
our website at www.constablerobinson.com.

No. of copies	Title	RRP	Total
	Hasty Death	£6.99	
	Snobbery with Violence	£6.99	
	Sick of Shadows	£6.99	
	Our Lady of Pain	£6.99	
	Grand total		£

FREEPOST RLUL-SJGC-SGKJ, Cash Sales Direct Mail Dept.,
The Book Service, Colchester Road, Frating, Colchester, CO7 7DW

Tel: +44 (0) 1206 255 800
Fax: +44 (0) 1206 255 930
Email: sales@tbs-ltd.co.uk

UK customers: please allow £1.00 p&p for the first book, plus 50p for
the second, and an additional 30p for each book thereafter, up to a
maximum charge of £3.00.

Overseas customers (incl. Ireland): please allow £2.00 p&p for the first
book, plus £1.00 for the second, plus 50p for each additional book.

NAME (block letters): _____

ADDRESS: _____

_____

_____ POSTCODE: _____

I enclose a cheque/PO (payable to 'TBS Direct') for the amount of

£ _____

I wish to pay by Switch/Credit Card

Card number: _____

Expiry date: _____ Switch issue number: _____